MUTANT MANTIS LUNCH LADIES!

A Monstertown Mystery

MUTANT MANTIS LUNCH LADIES!

A Monstertown Mystery

by Bruce Hale

DISNEP • HYPERION

Los Angeles   New York

First Edition, March 2017
1 3 5 7 9 10 8 6 4 2
FAC-029191-16344
Printed in Malaysia

Library of Congress Cataloging-in-Publication Data
Names: Hale, Bruce, author.
Title: Mutant mantis lunch ladies! : a Monstertown mystery / by Bruce Hale.
Description: First edition. | Los Angeles ; New York :
Disney-Hyperion, 2017 | Summary: Best friends Benny and Carlos risk
their lives to investigate when AJ reports seeing one of Monterrosa
Elementary's beloved lunch ladies change into a giant mantis.
Identifiers: LCCN 2015049809 | ISBN 9781484713242
Subjects: | CYAC: Monsters—Fiction. | Schools—Fiction. | Best Friends—
Fiction. | Friendship—Fiction. | Mutation (Biology)—Fiction. | School
lunchrooms, cafeterias, etc.—Fiction. | Mystery and detective stories.
Classification: LCC PZ7.H1295 Mut 2017 | DDC [Fic]—dc23
LC record available at https://lccn.loc.gov/2015049809

Reinforced binding
Visit www.DisneyBooks.com

For Jodi Hink and her cool kids

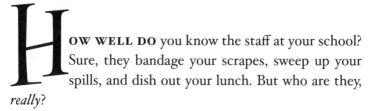

HOW WELL DO you know the staff at your school? Sure, they bandage your scrapes, sweep up your spills, and dish out your lunch. But who are they, *really*?

They seem like nice people.

But what if they're not?

What if they're secretly something much, much weirder?

Thanks to this suspicion, Benny Brackman and I found ourselves in the school kitchen one night, cowering behind a refrigerator door.

"*¡Ay, huey!*" I gasped. "What the heck was that?"

Benny peeked around the door toward the pantry in the corner. Nothing moved in the dimness.

"Don't ask me, Carlos," he said. "All I saw was you, running like mad. What did you see?"

"Freakity freaking freakiness!" I said. My heart hammered like a treeful of woodpeckers and my nerves jangled like wind chimes in a hurricane.

"Can you be more specific?" Benny asked, squinting into the dark.

"Too many arms, scary-fast, and it nearly took my head off. Where'd it go?"

I peered around Benny's shoulder. Although the open fridge did supply some yellowish light, its door faced the wrong way, back toward the deep fryer. My eyes were dazzled by brightness, which made the corner where the creature had ambushed me seem even darker.

"We should make sure what it is," whispered Benny.

"*You* make sure," I said. "That thing doesn't want us investigating the pantry, and I'm inclined to agree with it." Sweat popped out on my forehead.

Benny grumbled, but he gave in. We stared at the dark corner, we stared at the exit. All was quiet. Whatever it might be, the monster was motionless.

"Okay," I said, my throat dry, "we should go."

"You first," said Benny.

"No, you," I said. "I insist."

Licking his lips, Benny said, "Let's go together."

"Right."

The only problem with this plan was that the path to the exit ran much too close to the murky corner for comfort. My jaw clenched.

Nothing to it but to do it. My muscles tensed tighter than piano strings.

"On the count of three," said Benny. "One . . . two—"

"*Go!*" I yelled.

"What about three?"

We burst from behind the fridge with a wild cry, dashing straight for the door. As we tore past the food-prep island, something big stirred in the shadows to our left. Benny raised the can of Raid above his head and spritzed like he was writing the Declaration of Independence in the air.

Right away, my eyes stung. That sickly-sweet chemical smell filled my nose.

"Watch where you're spraying!" I cried.

Something scuttled behind us. My overactive imagination pictured ten million cockroaches picking up speed. I risked a glance back.

It was worse.

The world's biggest praying mantis was charging straight at us, wearing a hungry expression and an apron that read WHY YOU ALL UP IN MY GRILL?

Benny checked over his shoulder and his eyes grew wider than a sumo wrestler's waistband. With a strangled scream, he poured on the speed.

From behind us came an unnatural cry that I swear sounded like "Don't you dare leave that fridge door open!"

But I'm getting ahead of myself.

According to my teacher, Mr. Chu, you're supposed to grab your readers by the throat at the beginning of your story, but I feel like I'm just confusing you. You have no idea who Benny and I are, or why we're being chased through the kitchen by a giant bug.

And that's just not fair. (Both the confusion and the being chased, I mean.)

Let me back up a bit to where this story started. With the day Benny and I discovered what it really means to have a reputation as monster fighters.

Chapter One

Bugs and Kisses

I T ALL BEGAN with a note. We were sitting in class, playing Get Down with Decimals. Mr. Chu had just donned a purple Afro wig and cranked the disco music up to eleven-point-five. "Yeow, can ya feel the funky beat?" he yowled over the heavy thumping. "What's sixth-tenths in decimals . . . Tyler?"

Tyler Spork screwed up his face. "Um . . . uh, six-point-two?"

"Wrong-a-ding-dong," said our teacher. "Tina?"

"Zero-point-six," said Tina Green, the coolest girl in class, and a friend. (But not, you know, my *girl*friend.)

"Yeow!" said Mr. Chu.

"Disco sucks," Tyler whined.

Just then, a folded-up scrap of paper plopped onto my

desk. After I smoothed it out, the note read:

Can I talk to you guys at recess? It's _important_!!!
　　　　　　　　　　　　　　　　　　　—AJ

I glanced to my left. From the next row, AJ Banerjee gave me the pleading look of a kid who wants a puppy. He'd arrived late and been jumpy and distracted all morning, so I sent him a thumbs-up. AJ's look of relief was almost comical. But something—kids' intuition, maybe?—made me go _hmmm_.

Usually AJ just passed along the notes that my best friend, Benny Brackman, and I wrote to each other. Why was he sending _us_ a note?

I didn't have to wait long to find out.

After the bell rang, everyone got up to go. AJ waved us on, so Benny and I headed for the tetherball court. Then, before we could even start a game, our classmate came skulking across the playground like a double agent in a spy movie.

"Please, you've got to help me," he begged. His big brown eyes were as haunted as a Halloween movie marathon. His body practically quivered.

"No problem," said Benny. "The bathroom is right over there, third door on the left." He lifted the tetherball and gave it a whack.

"I'm not kidding," said AJ, wringing his hands.

"What is it, the heartbreak of head lice?" I said, trying to lighten his mood.

AJ's lips tightened. "This is serious." He looked left and right and then whispered, "I saw a bug."

I glanced at Benny. The puzzlement was mutual.

"Um, yeah, I see bugs every day," I said.

"This school is lousy with them," Benny agreed. "Stink bugs, cockroaches, you name it."

"No, a *giant* bug!" said AJ, eyes wild.

"What, like one of those Hercules beetles?" I asked, taking a swing at the tetherball. I'm no insect expert, but I know the freaky ones.

"Not a beetle," said AJ. "Mrs. Perez."

"The lunch lady?" I felt my forehead scrunch up in confusion. "I thought you said you saw a giant bug?"

"She is," he said.

Benny frowned. "Funny, but she does such a good impression of a human."

"Tricked me," I said.

With a frustrated growl, AJ clenched his fists. "Argh, I'm not explaining this right."

"No fooling," said Benny.

"Why don't you start at the beginning?" I said.

"Well, if you think it'll help," said AJ. "I was born in London almost ten years ago, the son of—"

"Not *that* beginning." Benny rolled his eyes. "Your problem?"

"Ah." AJ took a few moments to gather his thoughts. I would have suspected he was pranking us, but as far as

I could tell, he didn't have a sense of humor. "It started Friday," he said finally, "when the lunch ladies began giving Tenacity more responsibilities than me."

"Tenacity?" said Benny.

"The other head lunch monitor." AJ stopped while a bunch of third-grade girls blew past us, squealing. He continued, "That same day, all three lunch ladies started acting strangely."

"How strangely?" I asked.

He gazed off to the side. "Bullying me and the other boy monitors, acting cold. But the worst was when they started getting creepy."

"Creepy?" Benny perked up. He'd been zoning out, half watching the nearby basketball game. He's not big on long explanations.

"They gave me these weird fake smiles that made my skin crawl." AJ illustrated this with a fake smile of his own.

"Ooh, spooky!" Benny joked, smacking the tetherball again.

AJ flushed. "It *was*! But that's not all. This morning, Mrs. McCoy even pinched my arm."

"Um, on a scale of one to totally creepazoid, that barely registers," I said.

"Yeah, Carlos's grandma pinches me all the time." Benny grinned. "I'm a regular pinch-cushion." He looked for a reaction, but the joke sailed right over AJ's head.

Fact was, Benny and I knew creepy. We were becoming

experts on the subject, having saved our teacher from turning into a were-hyena earlier that same month.

"So where does the bug come in?" I asked.

Lowering his voice, AJ said, "I was bringing a stack of dishes into the kitchen after breakfast today, and my hands were greasy, so I dropped a plate."

"Did the lunch ladies give you twenty lashes?" asked Benny. I could tell he wasn't taking this seriously yet.

AJ ignored him. "Mrs. Perez was standing right there. She jumped at the noise, and for a split second, she changed."

"What do you mean?" I asked. Finally things were getting interesting.

AJ wrung his hands. "I—I know this sounds crazy, but for a moment, I could've sworn she turned into . . ."

"Into?" I asked, leaning forward.

"A giant bug," said AJ.

"A bug," I said.

"Exactly," said our classmate. "Antennae, wings, six legs—the whole deal."

"Let me get this straight." Benny cocked his head, squinting an eye. "You're saying one of our lunch ladies turned into some kind of humongous cockroach?"

"Cockroach, katydid, whatever," said AJ. "I don't know my insects."

"And then back into a human?" I asked.

"In the blink of an eye."

Some other kids waiting for a turn at tetherball gave us

funny looks, so Benny and I eased AJ off the blacktop and onto the grass.

"Have you been stressed out lately?" Benny asked him.

"No," he said.

"Needing glasses?" I asked.

"Never."

"Nuttier than a Christmas fruitcake?" asked Benny.

AJ glared at him. "I'm as sane as you, Benny Brackman."

I smirked. "That's not saying much."

AJ raised his palms. "I'm telling you both, I know what I saw. And I'm worried. Either I'm cracking up, or something truly strange is happening. Now will you help me find the truth or not?"

I blew out some air and took in the recess-related activities all around us. It seemed to be a normal day—blue skies, kids playing, yard-duty teachers gossiping. But as Benny and I knew too well, our school—heck, our whole town—was anything but normal. And sometimes people needed protecting from Monterrosa's weirdness.

"Why come to us?" asked Benny, acting indifferent. But I caught that sparkle in his eyes. He was hooked.

"I heard something about you two handling a were-hyena problem," said AJ.

"Just rumors," I said.

We hadn't discussed our supernatural experiences with anyone. It had felt great—heck, more than great—being the heroes and saving the day. But it wasn't the kind of thing you could mention to anybody. Not without getting sent to the funny farm.

In fact, the only people who knew the whole story were the ones who'd been there—Tina Green, Benny and me, and the comics-store owner, Mrs. Tamasese. I had kept quiet, and I was pretty sure Mrs. T wouldn't blab, so that left . . .

"I heard it from José, who got it from Gabi, who got it from Tina," said AJ.

Mystery solved. Tina was not the one to tell your secrets to.

"I guess word travels," said Benny. He seemed pleased.

"It sounded to me like you were the kind of guys who knew what to do when things got weird," said AJ. "And like you weren't afraid to lend a hand. Was I wrong?"

He was asking us to live up to our reputation as heroes. How often does *that* happen? I looked over at Benny. He raised an eyebrow and offered a crooked grin.

I rolled my eyes. This was probably a wild-goose chase, or else AJ was a better prankster than I thought. But still . . .

"Okay," I said. "How can we help?"

Chapter Two

If Cooks Could Kill

ONE OF THE problems with investigating a lunch lady was gaining access. If you wanted to see them up close and personal, you had to snoop before school, during morning recess, or at lunch.

That didn't leave a lot of time.

AJ offered to give us his allowance for a month just for helping to prove he wasn't crazy. Although Benny wanted to take it, I settled for one week's allowance and a plate of AJ's dad's famous chocolate-chip-oatmeal cookies. It seemed fairer, especially if this ended up being a case of too many scary movies and an overactive imagination.

With the deal made and only a few minutes of recess left, Benny and I hustled over to the cafeteria. The big room lay empty, the benches and tables already pulled out for lunchtime. It smelled of lemon floor cleaner, sloppy joes, and fresh hot-dog buns.

A clattering came from the kitchen. The pull-down steel grate that covered the serving counter was shut, so we headed for the door.

It suddenly struck me. "Wait, we need some kind of excuse," I said.

"What do you mean?" said Benny. "The cafeteria isn't off-limits."

"No, but we need a reason to visit the lunch ladies, or they'll get suspicious."

Benny didn't break stride. "Um . . ." He snapped his fingers. "Hunger. How's that?"

Checking the clock, I noticed time was running out like Halloween candy in November. "It'll have to do," I said.

He didn't even bother to knock. Benny just threw open the kitchen door.

"Hello, ladies!" he called, laying on the charm. "What's cooking for a couple of hungry boys?"

Mrs. Perez, Mrs. Robinson, and Mrs. McCoy all turned from their tasks and looked our way. Like the Three Bears, they ranged in size from big, to bigger, to biggest, with Mrs. Robinson topping the tall end of the scale at something over six feet. They seemed the same as always—like love and comfort in sensible shoes.

Same old hairnets, same old aprons.

The shortest and roundest, Mrs. McCoy, set a tray fresh

from the oven onto the steel counter. She casually stepped in front of it, watching us.

"Hello, boys," Mrs. Perez said in a stiff voice.

I eyed her closely. No wings, no extra legs. Gabi had always claimed that Mrs. Perez's blond hair was dyed, but if so, that seemed to be the only fake thing about her.

"Ooh, fresh cookies?" said Benny, heading for Mrs. McCoy's tray.

She held up a plump palm to stop him. "Not ready yet," she said flatly.

When Benny didn't even slow down, Mrs. Robinson stepped away from the sink and gripped his shoulder. "You should not be in here."

I edged sideways to see around them. The slender, crispy items lying on the tray didn't look like any sweet treats I'd ever seen. In fact, they reminded me of a Oaxacan dish my *abuela* had told me about.

"We were just looking for, um, a snack," I said.

"Snacks spoil meals." Mrs. Perez snagged Benny's elbow and steered him back toward the door, catching my arm along the way. "The kitchen is off-limits," she said, exhibiting all the charm of an alligator with a rash.

This wasn't like the Mrs. Perez I knew. She was a warm, motherly woman with a twinkly-eyed smile who would slip a kid a brownie every now and then.

"Having a bad day?" I asked.

Her head swiveled smoothly to regard me. "Not at all. It is a beautiful morning." She sounded as excited as a robot voice on a cell phone.

Something was definitely off.

But the oddest part came just after Mrs. Perez escorted Benny and me back into the cafeteria. Before releasing us, she gave us each a pinch on the upper arm, like someone testing the softness of a toilet-paper roll.

"Good day," she said, and turned to go.

"Adios," I replied.

"Yeah," said Benny. "Later."

The kitchen door locked behind her.

"So, that wasn't strange," said Benny, rubbing his arm where she'd pinched it.

"Or creepy," I said. "Did you get a look at what they were baking?"

Benny started for the exit. "Nah, but it smelled kinda nutty. What was it?"

I shook my head as we emerged back into the light of day. "I can't be sure, but it looked like . . . grasshoppers."

Benny grimaced. "Grasshoppers?"

"Yeah."

"No, that's not weird at all."

Before you go *What's so strange about cafeteria workers tossing kids out of the kitchen?*, let me fill you in about Monterrosa

Elementary's lunch ladies. Our cafeteria workers were some of the friendliest, most generous grown-ups at school.

Sure, they served up breakfast to kids who were on the free meal program. But if some other kid missed breakfast, they'd always make certain he or she didn't go hungry. Our lunch ladies were also generous with seconds. And they knew almost every kid's name, and asked about our families.

Some kids called them the Three Amigas: Gooey, Chewy, and Ratatouille. (It was a sign of affection.)

But the three women we'd just seen were nothing like that. They were (a) stingy, (b) cold, and (c) highly protective of their food. Plus they talked like a computer with a stick up its hard drive.

It was enough to make a guy wonder.

On our way back to the classroom after the bell rang, Benny and I bumped into AJ in the hallway. When he saw us, he rocked in place with pent-up energy.

"Well?" he said. "Did she turn into an insect?"

"Sorry, dude," said Benny, "she looked pretty normal to us."

AJ's shoulders slumped.

"No insect legs," I agreed. "But the lunch ladies weren't acting like themselves, that's for sure."

AJ's chin rose. "So you won't give up?"

"And miss out on your dad's cookies?" I said. "No way."

It did my heart good to see his spirits lift. Although I did think this was a waste of two top monster hunters like Benny and me. After all, nothing terribly strange or super-natural was going on here.

Just goes to show how wrong you can be.

Chapter Three

All You Need Is Lunch

OKAY, MAYBE THIS wasn't as exciting a problem as preventing our teacher from becoming a raving shapeshifter, but I have to confess something: three weeks past our first supernatural adventure, Benny and I had gotten a little bored.

You'd think that after tussling with a vicious were-hyena we'd be happy to live the life of normal kids. But here's the thing: facing up to monsters and saving your teacher (who remembered almost nothing of it) changes you.

Before all that happened, we'd been just your typical comics nerds—as plain as white rice on an ivory plate. But ever since we'd done brave things we didn't think we could do, Benny and I felt different. Even my parents started treating me like something special. (This drove my mini-diva of a little sister crazy. Another benefit.)

Truth is, after you've been a hero, it's hard to go back to being a nerd.

Maybe that explains why lunch period found us back at the cafeteria, investigating AJ's little problem. (That or the fact that neither of us was brown-bagging it that day.)

As we joined the line of kids waiting to be served, I noticed a commotion farther up the line. "What's going on?" I asked.

"Beats me," said Benny. "But they better not be running out of dessert."

Soon we found out. Just before we reached the serving area, we discovered that Mrs. Robinson was directing kids into two separate lines.

"Girls over here, boys over there," she kept repeating.

Whenever a boy would try to slip into the girls' line, she'd snag him by an arm and direct him back to the proper place. I noticed that none of the girls were trying to get in the boys' line. Either they were more obedient or they knew something we didn't.

"Separate meals? About time," said Benny. "Maybe this will cut down on the cootie factor."

"Somehow I don't think that's why they're doing it," I said.

"It's some new nutrition thing," said Tina Green, leaning

over from the next line. Everyone knew her as Karate Girl, although she had confessed to Benny and me that she'd never taken a lesson. She'd learned all her moves from Jackie Chan movies.

"What, boys need more nutrition 'cause we're so strong?" said Benny, flexing his spaghetti arm.

Tina eyed him skeptically. "Yeah, Brackman, that's gotta be it."

"Really?" he said.

"No," she said, rolling her eyes. "Way I heard it, boys and girls have different nutritional requirements."

"Because of our gnarly muscles," said Benny.

"Because we grow at different rates," said Tina.

Benny's smile wilted. "Oh." He turned to the lunch lady. "Mrs. Robinson, it's not fair that boys have to eat something different from girls."

Her stare would've frozen a polar bear. "Eat your lunch and do not complain."

I blinked. This wasn't like Mrs. Robinson at all.

"But—" Benny began.

"Move it!"

As we reached the serving area, I checked out the girls' choices. They had some kind of greenish glop, scrambled eggs, fish sticks, and a sloppy joe thing with the maybe-grasshoppers inside it. On the boys' side, we had hot dogs, french fries, lime Jell-O, cake, cookies, and brownies.

Benny opened his mouth to complain again, and I nudged him.

"Before you grumble, check out our lunch," I said.

His eyes widened. "Wow. I take that back, Mrs. Robinson—it's *very* fair!" Benny began piling his plate high with goodies.

"Hey!" Now it was Tina's turn to complain. "Why are they getting all the good stuff?"

Mrs. Robinson rested a hand on her shoulder. "We saved the good stuff for you—brain food, to help you reach your potential. Girl power!" She raised her fist in some kind of salute.

Tina grimaced. "Great, but can't we be powerful *and* have cake?"

The lunch lady frowned. "Cake makes you weak and fat."

"You say that like it's a *bad* thing," I said.

"Girls must stay strong, to rule." Mrs. Robinson's face lit with a fierce light. "Because we are the master ra—" She caught me staring and abruptly cut off her speech.

"But if cake makes you weak," said Tina, musing, "then why serve it to boys?"

The lunch lady flipped her hand in a dismissive gesture. "Who understands nutrition best, a schoolgirl or a trained professional? Eat your lunch."

She stepped away to police the lines, and Tina and I

scooped our respective lunches onto our trays. She cast a dubious look at her green glop.

"If you're nice, maybe I'll trade you a brownie," Benny told Tina. "Oh, wait—you've got nothing to trade." And he strutted off to our usual table, snickering.

"Don't mind him," I said. "He's sugar-mad."

Tina snorted. "Brackman? He's always been one french fry short of a Happy Meal." And she marched off to sit with Gabi and Cheyenne.

The younger grades were just finishing up their lunches and dropping off their trays as we came in. And wouldn't you know it, my little sister, Veronica, was among them.

"Hey, big brother!" Her eyes sparkled as she trotted over with a boy who'd recently joined her entourage.

I should explain. My six-year-old, starstruck sister is a brand-new actor on one of those Disney Channel series. She's got our mom's blond hair and a pair of huge dark eyes—even I have to admit she's pretty cute. But this week, when she was home for a break in filming, her normal brattiness was becoming pure obnoxiousness with her Hollywood-speak and her little fan club.

"Hey, Ron-Ron," I said, using her least favorite nickname.

She pouted for a split second, then her eyes went wide. "OMG, this cafeteria! Can you believe it? No dessert for girls! I can't *wait* to get back to LA. The Channel gives us *fabulous* lunches with *amazing* desserts."

"OMG," I said. "That's so awesome, I forgot to breathe."

As Veronica scowled, her little friend said "Hi" to me shyly.

"Hey, uh . . . Jacob?"

"Justin," he corrected. "What's it like to be related to someone so famous?"

"It's like riding a unicorn over a rainbow into a giant vat of candy," I said.

"Wow," he gushed. "It must be almost too much to take."

"You have no idea," I said.

Veronica tugged on his sleeve. "Come on, Justin. My fans are waiting! See you later, C-Man!"

"Not if I see you first," I teased.

By the time I joined Benny, he'd almost finished scarfing down his hot dog. "*Mmf*, AJ's cracked," he said through a mouthful. "I *like* the way the—*mmf*—lunch ladies are acting."

I munched my own lunch and stared off at Mrs. Robinson. She hadn't been her usual self—none of the lunch ladies had. "I don't know. . . ."

Benny stuffed some fries into his mouth. "Look, we didn't see any giant bugs, and the chow here is improving. I say we spend one more day on this, tell AJ we did our best, and collect our pay."

I frowned. "Is that what a hero would do?"

"Maybe not," said Benny, "but face it, Carlos. Not every situation is going to be chock-full of paranormal goodness."

"I guess," I said, half watching AJ at his lunch-monitor post. Just past him, Veronica was holding court with a bunch of girls while Justin carried their trays.

Benny took a bite of cake. "I wish something supernatural *was* happening, just to jazz up our lives. But sometimes things are just what they seem to be."

"Yeah, well, things seem weird to me," I said. "What about those grasshopper dealies I saw, and all that girl-power talk?"

"You think too much." Benny waved a fistful of fries at me. "Come on, Carlos, there's nothing paranormal going on. They're just making some changes."

"But—"

"Here's to nutrition!" Saluting me, Benny shoved all the fries into his mouth at once. Disgusting, but impressive.

"Carlos, Carlos!" Veronica appeared at my elbow. She shifted from foot to foot, biting her lip.

"What's wrong?" I asked. "Your makeup artist went on strike?"

"It's Justin," she said, her eyes as round as dark moons. "He's . . . disappeared."

Chapter Four

Missing? Impossible

"**J**USTIN'S GONE?**" I asked her. "Have you checked the playground? He probably got tired of waiting for you to finish autographing your fans' napkins."

"Nuh-unh." Veronica shook her head. "He didn't have time. I turned around, and he wasn't there."

"What do you want me to do about it?" I asked, taking a bite of brownie. Compared to the other things on my mind, this seemed like small change.

"Help me find him," she said. "I'm worried. Please?"

I blew out a sigh. "Be right back," I told Benny as I got up from the table. He grunted and kept stuffing his face.

Threading through the lunchtime traffic, I headed to where I'd noticed my sister standing earlier. "Where did you see him last?" I asked.

She pointed to a spot just ten feet away from the kitchen door.

"Okay," I said. "You go check the playground; I'll look around in here."

Veronica nodded. "Find him, okay? He's my friend."

I patted her shoulder. My sister may be a drama queen, but she is loyal to her subjects. Off she scampered to search outside.

Glancing around, I checked the busy cafeteria for the little guy. No sign of him. Most likely Justin had just ducked into the kitchen—maybe he was a lunch monitor like AJ. My sister was probably worried for nothing.

I poked my head through the kitchen doorway and rapped my knuckles on the half-open door. "Hello?"

One second, nobody was there, and the next, Mrs. McCoy loomed before me. I started.

"Do you require more food?" she said, in a voice as flat as a steamrolled flounder. "Help yourself—from the boys' side."

"Uh, no," I said, trying to look past her. "Actually . . . did a second grader named Justin come this way?"

"Of course not." Mrs. McCoy smoothly shifted to block my view. "The kitchen is off-limits to students."

"Even lunch monitors?" I asked.

"We have no second-grade lunch monitors."

I tried peering past her the other way, and she shifted again without seeming to move. All I caught was a glimpse of Mrs. Perez's back.

"I could've sworn . . ." I said.

"Swearing is against school rules," she said. "Now I must return to work." Her smile didn't reach her eyes. "Bye-bye."

The door shut so quickly I had to hop backward to avoid getting my nose smacked. If I'd had spider-sense like Peter Parker, it would have been tingling.

Benny glanced up when I returned to our table. "What's going on?"

"Veronica's friend just vanished," I said. "I think something's fishy."

"Yeah, the girls' lunch," Benny said, popping the last of his french fries into his mouth.

I put a fist on my hip. "Weren't you the one moaning about nothing supernatural going on? Mrs. McCoy said the kid isn't in the kitchen, but she was acting strange."

"Okay, okay." He raised his palms. "We'll check it out." Benny surveyed my half-eaten food. "You going to finish that brownie?"

I shook my head, and he practically inhaled the treat.

As we headed out the exit, AJ caught my eye from his post across the room. He spread his hands and raised his eyebrows in a question. I gave him a reassuring nod. In truth, I felt far from reassured. I didn't know if I was imagining it or if odd things were really going on.

Did I want bad stuff to happen just so Benny and I could play hero? And if so, did that make me a bad guy?

Outside, the overcast skies pressed down like an iron on a wrinkled shirt. Kids were doing their usual carefree kid stuff, but I had heavier things on my mind.

In a flurry of arms and legs, Veronica came running up. "Did you find him?"

"Nope," I said. "You?"

Her shoulders sagged. "No."

"Don't worry, I'll keep looking. You too."

She nodded and dashed off again.

Benny and I walked around the cafeteria to the kitchen side, keeping an eye out for Justin. Not a trace. The kitchen windows were too high to see through, even taking a running jump.

"Help me drag that trash can over," said Benny. After dumping the contents of the can into the recycling container (I could picture our teachers' disapproving frowns), we set it upside down beneath the window. I glanced about nervously, but no one was watching.

With a boost from me, Benny climbed on top of the can. When he peeked through the pane, he flinched back with a startled "Eeugh!"

"What is it?" I asked. "Are they filleting the kid?"

"Worse," said Benny. "These windows are *filthy*!"

"Be serious."

"I am. You could catch a disease just by touching them."

I sighed. "Do you see the kid? Or the lunch ladies?"

"Dude, I can't see anything," he said, climbing down.

"They could be holding a hoedown with dancing heifers in there and I wouldn't have a clue."

Casting about for another way in, I noticed a side door farther down the building. "Let's try over there."

We replaced the trash can and headed for the door. When we were about five feet away, it swung open, and a strange woman stepped out. (I don't mean that she had three eyes or purple hair or anything; she was just a stranger.)

"Oh," said the woman, a little surprised. She looked like any other mom you'd see around school—pretty, pony-tailed, medium-old, and dressed in a red polo shirt and khaki pants.

"Excuse us," I said, trying to step around her to the door.

She closed it behind her. "You can't go in there."

"Why not?" asked Benny, with his most innocent smile. "You did."

Mrs. Ponytail's lips clamped into a thin line. Amazingly, she was invulnerable to my friend's charm. "I," she said, "happen to be the chair of the PTA lunch committee. And who, exactly, are you?"

"We're, uh, the official cafeteria taste testers," said Benny. "We're all about the spice."

She wasn't amused.

I tried to look harmless. (It was pretty much my regular expression.) "We just wanted to talk to Mrs. Perez."

"Oh? What about?" The mom crossed her arms.

"Um . . ." I glanced at Benny.

"That's between us and Mrs. Perez," he said. "Private business. About . . . you know, testing tastes."

Pulling a key ring from her pocket, Mrs. Ponytail turned and locked the door.

I snuck a glance at Benny. *Taste testing?* I mouthed. He shrugged.

The lady rounded on us. "I'll thank you not to bother the cafeteria staff."

"But what about our private business?" asked Benny. "For all you know, this could be a flavor emergency!"

"If you don't move along," she said, glowering, "you'll learn what a real emergency is." Her fist clenched at her side, and her gaze was hot enough to fry bacon.

"Is that a no?" said Benny.

"Come on, Benny," I said, pulling him away. "I think we were just threatened."

He sniffed. "Man, the PTA has really gone downhill."

We shuffled away from the building, followed by Mrs. Ponytail's suspicious stare. Who knew PTA moms could be so tough? Finally she got tired of watching us and went off to handle her own business.

Benny and I stopped on the blacktop, looking back at the kitchen.

"You heard the lady," he said. "Nothing else we can do to help your sister. Right, Carlos?"

I wasn't quite ready to give up. But that wasn't what distracted me. My attention had been caught by some kind of skylight or vent on the roof, just above the kitchen.

"Carlos?"

My eyes traced the roofline over to a huge spreading fig tree whose branches overhung it. "There's one more thing we can try," I said.

Benny followed my gaze. "Really? You want to climb up there in broad daylight? I thought *I* was the reckless one."

"Fine," I said, heading for the tree. "You don't want to come, then keep watch."

I didn't know what had gotten into me. Usually I'm the voice of reason, the guy who overthinks things. Maybe little Justin reminded me of Veronica, who I sometimes picked on but would defend to the death. Maybe I was just feeling stubborn.

Trailing after me, Benny said, "I didn't say I wasn't coming. We'll just have to be sneaky, that's all."

We loitered by the tree, which luckily was behind the building, partly shielded from sight. When Benny and I were sure no grown-ups were watching, we scaled the trunk. Just as we reached the lowest branch, I noticed a teacher on yard duty looking our way.

"Freeze!" I whispered.

Benny and I clung to the thick branch, barely breathing. Were there enough leaves to cover us?

The teacher took a step toward us. But then two kids

got into a fight over a basketball, and he hurried off to break it up. We resumed our scramble upward.

In no time we scaled the rest of the gnarled branches and stepped onto the roof. It smelled of tar and rotting fruit from the tree. Several Frisbees, a baseball cap, and a bunch of mismatched sneakers decorated its rough, tar-papered surface.

Benny picked up the purple flying disk. "I forgot all about this one," he said.

"I told you you couldn't throw it all the way over," I said. "But would you listen?"

Benny grinned. "Never." He chucked his Frisbee off the side.

"Are you nuts?" I asked, grabbing him and pulling him down. "Do you *want* to get caught?"

His grin turned apologetic. "Don't worry. People never look up."

I peered over the edge. A couple of kids had noticed the Frisbee land. One of them glanced at our rooftop, and I ducked back out of sight.

"Don't stand," I said, "and don't toss anything else off. Okay?"

"Yeah, yeah," said Benny.

Together we crept across the stubbly surface of the roof, toward the hatchlike opening above the kitchen. When we were right up beside it, we lay flat on the warm tar paper, making doubly sure we weren't spotted.

Thump, bump, clitter, clatter, whoosh.

The sound of water running and trays banging rose through the skylight. We listened a while. Unfortunately, the lunch ladies didn't say anything like "Good thing we got that second grader out of sight" or "I wonder if little Justin would taste better with potatoes or carrots?"

All we heard besides the cleaning-up sounds were some clicks and whirs—probably the dishwasher doing its thing.

Benny's not the most patient guy in the world. Or even the second most patient. Before I knew what was happening, he'd crawled up to the very edge and was trying to peek under the Plexiglas bubble that covered the hatch.

I tugged on his T-shirt. "Get back!" I whispered.

He made a little "unh" sound of surprise.

Instantly, the clatter below us stopped. I grimaced. Had they heard us? Or even worse, spotted Benny?

Something hissed below, like the world's biggest alley cat. A softer *tuk-tuk-tuk* answered it, like two machines having a conversation. Then, nothing.

We froze, as still as moonlight shining on a monument.

After a long pause, the clicks and whirs started up again, slower and quieter than before. I let out my breath. When Benny twisted to look at me, I made a "let's go" gesture.

Together, we crept back across the roof, rising to a half crouch when we were far enough away from the vent.

"Did they see you?" I hissed as we clambered into the branches.

"I don't think so," said Benny, "but I—"

"Hey, you kids!" a man's voice boomed from below. "Come down from there, right now!"

Chapter Five

Boo in the Face

MY SHOULDERS tensed and my jaw clenched tighter than an Olympian's spandex. Busted! I glanced over at Benny.

"Hold still," he whispered from the next branch over. "Maybe he can't see us."

"I can totally see you," said the voice from below. "No use trying to hide."

Shoot.

Maybe I should've been more like myself and less like Benny. Maybe I shouldn't have led us up onto the roof after all.

Too late now. With sinking hearts, we made our way down the branches to the trunk, dropping onto the ground in front of a familiar figure.

"Dudes," he said.

It was Mr. Decker, Monterrosa Elementary's new head custodian. Known among the students by his nickname of Malibu (or Boo, for short), Mr. Decker looked like a cross between an aging surfer and an unmade bed that had been left outside too long. His golden haystack hair was scattered with gray, and his tan face had more wrinkles than a shar-pei pup.

"Hi, Mr. Decker," Benny and I mumbled, studying the ground.

"What were you dudes doing up there?" said the custodian. "You know the roof is off-limits."

"We, uh . . ." I noticed he was holding Benny's disk. "We were getting Benny's Frisbee back."

"Yeah," said Benny, picking up my cue. "I bet Carlos I could throw it all the way over the building, and I, uh, lost."

Mr. Decker wagged his head. "I can respect a man's attachment to his Friz. But that roof is dangerous. If you went splat, your moms and dads would sue the school district, and the Boo would be out of a job."

I wasn't quite sure what he was talking about, but an apology seemed in order. "Sorry, Mr. Decker."

"I mean, the Beatles say all you need is lunch, but a paycheck sure comes in handy."

"We're really *really* sorry," said Benny, laying on the blue-eyed charm. "Promise we won't do it again."

The custodian scratched one leathery cheek with the Frisbee. "Afraid I'm gonna have to report you."

"No!" cried Benny, genuinely alarmed. If he got into any more trouble, his police-detective father might lock him up and throw away the key. And I'd probably be in there with him.

"Please don't," I added. "We've learned our lesson, I promise. Please don't tell Mrs. Johnson."

For a long moment, the custodian eyed us both. He glanced off at the playground, thinking. "Here's the thing," he said at last. "I get pie with a little help from my friends."

"Huh?" I said. Sometimes grown-ups made no sense at all.

"It's a song quote." He gestured toward the grass. "It means I've got a lot of trash to pick up before lunch period is over. If someone *volunteered* to help, I might be able to overlook a little rule violation."

Relief pinkened Benny's cheeks. "That's great!" he said. "Thanks, Mr. Decker."

"Please," said the rangy custodian, "call me Mr. Boo. Mr. Decker's my grandfather."

"Not your father?" asked Benny.

"Nah," said the custodian. "Him we call Lulu."

I blinked.

"Okay, Mr. Boo," I said. "We're volunteering."

Leading Benny and me back to his cart, the custodian returned Benny's Frisbee and handed each of us a trash bag. We set to work on an area near the chain-link fence that kids had somehow mistaken for a garbage can. After a few minutes of stuffing the bag with candy wrappers, empty milk cartons, and other junk, a thought struck me.

"Hey," I said to Benny, "I've got an idea."

"There's a first time for everything."

"Ha ha." I jerked my head at the custodian. "He spends a lot of time in the lunchroom. Maybe he could tell us if the cafeteria ladies are up to anything weird."

"Genius!" he said. "Oh, Mr. Boo?"

The custodian stabbed a soda can with his trash spear, spun the pole, and flipped the can into his bag of recyclables. A true artist. "What's up?" he said.

"Carlos and I were wondering," said Benny, "have you noticed anything . . . different about the lunch ladies lately?"

"Different?" The grizzled surfer cocked his head. "Like how?"

"Oh, you know," I said, "acting differently, talking differently?" Kidnapping little kids for evil purposes?

"Not really," he said. "Lately they're not as quick to hook a janitor up with a doughnut, but maybe that's part of their whole nutrition thing."

"Yeah, what's the deal with that?" asked Benny.

Mr. Boo lifted a shoulder. "Search me. It just started today—you'd have to ask Mrs. Johnson. Heee-*yah*!" He whirled like a kung fu master, expertly spearing a carton, three pieces of notepaper, and an apple core. Into his trash bag they went.

Benny and I returned to our own trash collecting (with a lot less style). But just as we were getting into the rhythm of it, I heard a familiar voice.

"Hey, check this out. It's Dumb and Dumber on trash patrol!"

It was Tyler Spork and his sidekick, Big Pete—the last people I wanted to see right now—or ever.

Pete laughed, a *hork-hork-hork* sound like a seal choking on a fish bone. "Benny and Carlos are in trouble," he crowed. "What'd you do to get community service?"

I cringed.

Benny said, "Not that it's any of your business, but we volunteered to help."

"Sure you did," said Tyler. "'Cause you just *love* trash."

"Not really," said Benny. "We've eaten your mom's cooking before."

Tyler snarled, clenching a fist. But when Mr. Boo straightened and gave him a hard stare, he turned and nudged Big Pete. "Come on. Let's go someplace that's not so stinky."

"Hey, dudes," Mr. Boo said to us once the jerks were out of earshot, "no vermin!"

"What?" At first I thought he was referring to the absence of Tyler and Pete.

"I just remembered something odd about the kitchen and cafeteria," he went on.

"Oh yeah?" I said. "What's that?"

"It's bug-free," said Mr. Boo.

Was he referring to the giant insect AJ saw? "You mean . . ."

"Let me explain." The custodian leaned his spear against the fence and gathered his long hair back into a rubber band. "I've always had to set traps for mice and roaches, right? Wherever there's food, those little buggers line up for a taste."

"Um, yeah." Benny and I exchanged a disgusted look, imagining our lunch being sampled by pests.

"But yesterday, all the traps were empty. No bugs, no rodents."

"No fooling?" said Benny.

"Almost like they got scared off or something," the custodian mused, looking unnerved. Then he shook himself like a shaggy dog at the beach and went back to his usual mellow manner. "Anyways, that's all I can think of. Why do you wanna know?"

"Oh," said Benny, "we're, uh . . ."

"We're big fans of food service," I said. "And we just wanted to make sure that our favorite lunch ladies were feeling okay."

"Yeah," said Benny. "What he said."

Mr. Boo gave us a funny look, then nodded and went back to collecting trash. But all that ran through my mind until the bell released us was this: Cockroaches are tough enough to survive nuclear war, right? So what in the world would be scary enough to frighten them off?

Chapter Six

Float Like a Butterfly, Sting Like E.T.

R. CHU ALWAYS says to leave out the boring stuff when telling a story. Mostly I try. I mean, who wants to read about who pulled whose hair or what homework we got, or who picked his nose and got caught (Tyler Spork, for the record)?

But a couple of small things happened in class that afternoon that made my spider-sense tingle.

First, not long before second recess, Mrs. Johnson's voice came over the PA system. "Attention, students: We're looking for Justin Delgado. If anyone has seen him since lunchtime, please tell your teacher."

"Anyone?" said Mr. Chu. We all shook our heads. Benny gave me a troubled look.

Second, not long after that, some of the girls started acting a little . . . different. Mr. Chu had split us up into groups to discuss ecosystems. My group had Tina, Amrita, Zizi, and AJ in it. Poor AJ seemed jumpier than a tree frog in a bouncy castle.

"Find anything yet?" he muttered as we pulled our desks together.

"Nothing solid," I said.

He gritted his teeth. "Hurry. This is really starting to freak me out."

"Don't worry," I said. "We're on the case."

Overhearing us, Amrita laughed. "You *are* a case," she said.

My mouth gaped like a train tunnel, I was so stunned. Amrita is that girl in your class who always looks perfect, never sasses the teacher, and acts more like a grown-up than the grown-ups. But here she was, back-talking like Benny.

"Well, he *is* a boy," said Tina, nastily. "And boys are pretty pathetic—especially Carlos." The girls cackled together.

Stung, I rocked back in my seat. You expect a little ribbing from your friends, but that crossed the line into downright mean. Before I could respond, Tina started our discussion by mentioning how much healthier our ecosystems would be if women were running the country. Zizi and Amrita agreed, and we were off and running.

But the whole time, Tina's comment stayed with me, like a splinter under the skin.

When school let out, Benny and I trotted over to Amazing Fred's Comix and More, known to most of Monterrosa as the comics store. Not only was it one of our favorite after-school hangouts, but we had some questions for its owner, Mrs. Tamasese. And not just "In which issue does Spider-Man first meet Doc Ock?" Besides being a comics lover and former pro wrestler, Mrs. T was something of an expert on the strange and supernatural.

When we stepped into the cool interior of the long, low shop, a few bars of the Indiana Jones theme song played. No matter what mood I was in, it always made me feel more like a hero. Decorated with colorful murals of monsters and superheroes, the store was stuffed to the gills with comics, graphic novels, games, magician supplies, and even some books on the paranormal.

A handful of middle school kids were rooting through the graphic novels. Mrs. Tamasese sat by herself at the glass counter, a comics queen, ruler of all she surveyed.

"Howzit, boys!" she called.

"Hey, Mrs. T," we answered, joining her. Under the glass in front of her lay the expensive stuff—original Pokémon cards, rare baseball cards, and issues of comics like The

Ultimate Spider-Man No. 1 and Cerebus the Aardvark No. 1—which she swore were worth big bucks.

"Looking for the newest Hulk?" she asked Benny. "I hear that bugger got himself in some real trouble this time." The former "Samoan Slammer" always tended to talk about comic-book characters like they were old wrestling buddies of hers.

"Uh, no," he said, glancing around to see if anyone was near enough to overhear. "We actually need to talk about the *other* stuff."

Mrs. Tamasese's eyebrows rose. "Ahh," she said, leaning forward in her souped-up purple wheelchair. "The freaky-kine stuff. Lay it on me."

I told her what we had so far—the lunch ladies acting strangely, their cooking what looked like grasshoppers, AJ's glimpse of a giant insect, the disappearing pests, and the vanished second grader. It wasn't much, but it was kind of creepy.

"Oh, Carlos, I forgot to tell you," Benny added. "You know when I looked through the vent, up on the roof?"

"Yeah?"

"I caught a peek of the lunch ladies talking, but it was so weird."

"What was?" I asked.

"It almost seemed like, instead of talking, they were communicating in clickety-clack."

My stomach plummeted like a turtle taking flying lessons. "Uh, that's not good."

"What's clickety-clack?" asked Mrs. Tamasese.

We explained how we'd heard clicks, clacks, hisses, and whirs when we were eavesdropping from the roof. The store owner leaned back in her chair, fiddling with her puka-shell necklace.

"People that look like giant bugs," she mused. "People that communicate in click-clack. Hmm . . ."

"What does it mean?" I asked, fidgeting.

"It means . . . 'hmm,'" she said.

Benny rolled his eyes.

Mrs. Tamasese paused to ring up a middle-grade girl buying a graphic novel of *Usagi Yojimbo*, some kind of samurai rabbit. Benny and I shifted from foot to foot until they were done. Then the store owner wheeled her way through the gap in the counter and crooked a finger.

"This way, guys."

She rolled along at a good clip, her broad shoulders bunching and flexing under her shirt. Mrs. T may have been retired from wrestling, but she still looked like a superhero from the waist up. She stopped in the paranormal section.

"Carlos, grab that blue book on the highest shelf," said Mrs. Tamasese.

I stretched and pulled down the book she wanted. *"Aliens Among Us?"* I said. What the heck?

Flipping through the pages, she stopped at one spread.

"Ah," said the store owner. "Here we go. . . ."

Benny and I came close, peering over her shoulders. Her finger had landed on an illustration showing a slender creature with a big, triangular head, huge eyes, and stubby antennae.

"So you're saying . . ." I began. An awful feeling crept over me, like spiders under the skin.

"There's more than one thing that resembles a giant bug."

I looked at Benny. Benny looked at me.

"But . . . aliens?" His chuckle sounded forced. "You don't really believe in aliens, do you?"

Mrs. Tamasese's laugh was as full and rich as a river of chocolate syrup. "Believe? Let's just say I'm not someone who stays up all night watching for UFOs and painting WELCOME, EXTRATERRESTRIALS! on my roof. But I *do* believe in the *possibility* of aliens."

I squeezed my eyes shut for a moment. Aliens at Monterrosa Elementary? My brain was as muddled as a Mongolian spy movie without subtitles.

Mrs. T laughed again. "Look at you two, like a couple of stunned mullets. You've seen actual were-hyenas."

"Yeah . . ." said Benny, gnawing a fingernail.

"Then why are aliens so hard to swallow?"

"Um, I guess it's . . . possible," I said. My limbs felt shaky. I didn't know which was worse, huge hungry insects or evil aliens on a mission. If they caught us, would they take us to their leader or fry us on the spot?

Benny's face looked paler than usual. "So, uh, if they're aliens, how are they impersonating our lunch ladies?"

The store owner spread her hands. "If they were giant bugs, how would they be doing it?"

He cocked his head. "In other words, who knows?"

"In other words," Mrs. T agreed.

"Whatever the heck they are," I said, "we need to do two things."

"Bag 'em and tag 'em?" asked Benny, trying to muster some bluster.

I shook my head. "First, find out whether they really *are* impersonating our cooks, and why. Second, locate the real lunch ladies."

A boy's voice cut in on our discussion. "A little help over here?" one of the middle schoolers hollered from the counter.

"Duty calls," said Mrs. Tamasese, pushing the alien book into my hands and pointing to the shelf. "Good luck, boys. Let me know if you want to talk about it some more. I love this stuff."

We watched her roll smoothly away, then plunked ourselves down and flipped through the section of the book she'd showed us. Benny and I read about aliens abducting humans, aliens dissecting humans, aliens using us like cattle.

It began to give me a serious case of the oojie-woojies.

"Anything helpful?" Benny asked. "Anything about how to stop 'em?"

"Nope. Just this: 'There are good aliens and bad aliens, so if you meet one, try to learn its intentions.'"

"Brilliant," said Benny. "I'll be sure to ask them while they're slicing me open." He shivered. "Now I'll never get to sleep tonight."

I placed *Aliens Among Us* back on the shelf next to *I Married an Alien*. "What now?" I asked.

"Now?" said Benny. "Now we come up with a brilliant plan. And pronto."

"A plan," I said, rubbing my chin, "involves heavy thinking."

A weak grin began to break through Benny's worried expression. "And heavy thinking calls for . . ."

"Brain food!" we said together.

"Great minds think alike," I said, leading the way out of the comics store.

Benny nodded. "And fools rarely disagree."

Chapter Seven

You Can Lead a Boy to Nachos, But You Can't Make Him Think

SOME PEOPLE TRY to tell you that fish is brain food. That's a bunch of baloney. For sheer inspiration and mental stimulation, I've found that few things on Earth can match my *abuela*'s chicken mole nachos.

When Benny and I blew through the front door at my house, something that sounded like a goose with a sinus infection was honking out Bob Marley's "Three Little Birds." I know the song—and that noise—because my grandma plays sax for a ska band called Marley's Ghost. It's kinda cool and kinda weird at the same time. But my dad says it keeps her out of trouble.

"Abuelita, we're home!" I called.

Instantly, my shaggy dog, Zeppo, galumphed into the room and leaned against me, wagging his tail—his signal that he wanted to be scratched behind the ears. I obliged him.

"*¡Hola, mijo!*" Abuelita called. "Just let me finish this riff."

A few honks, a squeak, and a snort later, she appeared in the living room doorway carrying a golden saxophone. Abuelita lives with us during the week while my mom is down in LA with Veronica. On those days, I miss my mom something fierce, but to be honest, my grandma is the better cook. This week they were both here, because Veronica was home on hiatus—that's Hollywood talk for a short break in filming.

After her usual kiss and hug, Abuelita said, "Your mother's off running errands with your sister. Are you boys hungry?"

"Always," said Benny.

"We're working on an important project," I said. "Any chance of some nachos with the leftover chicken mole?"

"Mmm, mole," said Benny, perking up.

She beamed. "It'll be ready before you know it."

We always have snacks over at my place and not Benny's because his mom only offers the kind of healthy snacks that contain no molecules of actual food in them.

Zeppo followed Benny and me into the family room and flopped down on the floor. We did searches for *aliens in Monterrosa* and *giant bugs in Monterrosa* on my dad's computer. (Mr. Chu would've been proud of our research skills.)

Unfortunately, we didn't turn up anything that was useful. Our giant-bug search uncovered insect-collecting articles from the natural history museum, a photo of a titan beetle (as big as your face!), and a review of Hotel Monterrosa that mentioned someone finding a huge cockroach in the bathroom.

The alien search results weren't any better—just a blurry video of a UFO that might have been a motorcycle headlight, and a letter to the editor complaining about the newspaper using the words "illegal aliens" in a headline. (As someone whose grandma moved here from Mexico before she was an American citizen, I had to agree with the letter writer. Abuelita was no alien. She may be a little unusual, but she didn't come in a spaceship.)

While we worked, the house began smelling better and better. Finally, Abuelita showed up with a massive plate of nachos, and we took a break. Several bites of cheesy goodness later, I realized two things: (a) my *abuela* was a truly awesome cook, and (b) why do a web search when we had a longtime Monterrosa resident in the same room?

"Hey, Abuelita?" I said.

She looked up from rubbing Zeppo's belly. "Hmm?"

"We're doing this, um, report on aliens and giant bugs in Monterrosa." I glanced at Benny, uncomfortable about fibbing to her.

He crunched down on another cheese-drenched chip. "Yeah, and we're not really getting anywhere."

I scratched my cheek. "I was wondering, have you ever heard of aliens in Monterrosa?"

"Aliens?" Abuelita ruffled the thick fur on Zeppo's chest. "I think the way they say it these days is 'undocumented immigrants.'"

"No, the other kind," said Benny. "Like E.T.?"

My grandma snorted out a laugh. "Seriously? A few years back, a couple of people claimed they saw UFOs. But it was just airplanes."

"Okay, scratch aliens," I said. "How about great big bugs?"

"Like *las cucarachas*?" Her eyes twinkled.

"Bigger than cockroaches," I said.

"*Really* big bugs," Benny added. He spread his arms as wide as he could, a nacho chip in each hand.

Abuelita stood and stretched. She frowned slightly as she stared out the window.

"What is it?" I asked.

"It's crazy," she said.

Benny glanced over at me. "We're used to crazy," he said.

"We've spent a lot of time there," I added.

Dipping a chip into her own gooey concoction, my *abuela*

said, "It's just a rumor—and an old one, from twenty-five years ago."

"Well?" I prompted.

She nibbled thoughtfully. "Back before that old army base closed, some people used to say they were doing experiments with insects out there."

"With insects?" said Benny. "What, like trying to cross a pill bug with a tank?"

Abuelita chuckled. "Who knows? We had no proof— just rumors of giant bugs."

"That's all?" I asked.

Her eyebrows lifted. "Oh, I almost forgot. My friend Elena once claimed that she saw an ant the size of a coyote running off with someone's pet cat."

I sat up straight.

Benny's eyes got big. "Wow. Really?"

My *abuela* shrugged. "Of course, Elena also claimed that she was secretly going out with Robbie Dungworth, but that was just *tonterías*—nonsense. Robbie was secretly going out with me."

Benny and I just gaped.

She popped the rest of the chip into her mouth. "Enjoy!" And with that, Abuelita strolled off to continue practicing.

"Wow," Benny repeated.

"You said it." I rubbed my jaw. "I don't know which is weirder—rumors of giant ants or my *abuela* dating someone named Robbie Dungworth."

"Do you think there really could be huge insects out there?"

"Who knows?" I said.

Since it was getting late and so far Benny and I had uncovered only spooky rumors and unsettling tales, we decided to revisit the whole thing later. In the meantime, we dedicated ourselves to polishing off the nachos.

Hey, even heroes deserve a break every now and then.

By the time we reached the last cheesy clumps, Benny and I had seriously slowed down. We sprawled on the sofa with the platter between us and Zeppo at our feet.

Studying the cheese dangling off a chip in his hand, Benny said, "Back at the comics store, you said something."

"I do that sometimes. Which something do you mean?"

"Before we figure out whether the lunch ladies are bugs or aliens or garden gnomes, we first have to prove that they're not really themselves."

I set my uneaten chip back down on the platter. "That sounds like me."

Benny gently thwacked his cheese strand and watched it sway. "I think I may have figured out a way to do that."

Too stuffed to eat another bite, I said, "Ugh, must you play with your food?"

"That's it exactly," said Benny.

"Huh?"

And then he told me his plan.

Chapter Eight

Foodfellas

THE KEY TO any successful food fight is finding the right participants. Victims won't fight back. And bullies? They'll just whack you over the head with a tray and stuff a hot dog in your ear.

At lunchtime the next day, after loading up with junk food on the boys' side of the serving line, Benny and I carefully chose a table with more guys than girls. I know, I know. As Tina would probably remind me, girls can food-fight just as well as boys. But in my experience, they're not nearly as willing to get messy.

Benny and I sat across from each other, to maximize our target coverage. We checked that AJ had gotten his fellow lunch monitors occupied in helping him with some bogus problem. (He wasn't thrilled, but he went along with us.)

And then we went to work.

"No way could Thor beat Superman in a fair fight," snapped Benny.

"Come on!" I said. "Superman is just some dude in tights. Thor is a god!"

"Oh yeah?" Benny snarled. "He doesn't have super speed."

I faked being offended. "Oh no? Thor can swing his hammer at *twice* the speed of light, but Superman can only move at ninety-nine percent of it. Suck on that, Spandex Boy!"

"You doodle-brained mouth breather!" Benny cried, half rising from the bench. He grabbed a chunk of lasagna,

cocked his arm, and let fly, deliberately missing me. It flew to the next table.

Splat! went the casserole against the back of Aiden's head.

"You bubbleheaded ding-dong!" I cried, launching the Jell-O from my plate. It soared past Benny and spattered into Egberto's face.

"Food fight!" Benny bellowed, leaping up onto our table. He turned, scooped, and sent a fistful of cookie nuggets sailing at the kids to his left.

"Food fight!" I answered, hurling bite-size brownies at the kids on the right.

True to the scientific law of action and reaction (See? I do pay attention during science lessons), Aiden, Egberto, and the other kids who'd been hit sounded their war cries and fired back. I took a lasagna clump to the forehead, and Benny was brained by an oatmeal cookie.

With whoops and squeals, the lunchroom erupted into a free-for-all of waving arms and flying food. It was as if someone had turned off the gravity, and everyone's lunches began floating through the air.

Jell-O jumped, lasagna levitated, and french fries flew. I saw Amrita splattered with succotash and Cheyenne drenched in gravy. I saw several fifth graders bombarded by spinach casserole.

All well and good. All as planned.

But what I didn't expect was the good girls—girls like Amrita, Cheyenne, and Zizi—joining the fight with total gusto. They hooted and hollered as loud as the boys, flinging food left and right. I took a cheese enchilada in the face from Gabi, who hurled it with glee.

So much for girls being cleaner.

Tugging on Benny's T-shirt, I shouted over the din, "Can you see them? What are they doing?"

The whole point of our food fight (aside from pure fun) was to see how the cafeteria workers would react. If they responded with horror, shock, and anger, we'd know they were themselves.

But if they reacted differently? That would tell a tale.

From his post atop the table, Benny scanned the mob, searching for the lunch ladies. I could tell when he spotted them by the way his face scrunched up.

"What?" I yelled.

He pointed. "See for yourself."

When I climbed up to join him, I spotted AJ in the corner, shaking his head in dismay. I looked farther and felt my own face crinkle in confusion. "Huh?"

As we stood watching (and occasionally getting hit by food), we saw Mrs. Perez and Mrs. McCoy going from table to table. They didn't lift a finger to stop the boys—in fact, they completely ignored us. But with every girl they met, the lunch ladies gently but deliberately took her lunch away.

All the while, gusts of grub sailed past them like an edible hurricane.

"Weird," said Benny. "They're punishing the girls by taking away their food."

"So much for girl power," I said. But then I noticed Mrs. Perez ducking down and scraping some of the girls' thrown lunches onto a separate tray she carried.

"What's she doing?" said Benny.

A thought struck me. "They care about girls' food, but not boys' food," I said. "What's up with that?"

Benny shrugged. "Beats me."

"Well, I think we've proved one thing for sure."

"How easy it is to start a food fight?" said Benny, wiping a smear of tomato paste off his cheek.

"That," I said, "and that these are not our normal lunch ladies."

Later that same lunch period, we found ourselves sitting on visitors' chairs covered with newspaper outside the principal's office. (The paper came courtesy of the school secretary, Mrs. Garcia, who said she didn't fancy cleaning lasagna off the upholstery. Go figure.)

Sure, we were aware of the risks of starting a food fight. And now it was time to face the music. As I knew too well from comic books and movies, heroes always ended up paying the price.

Stern as a sheriff facing down gunslingers, Mrs. Johnson loomed in her office doorway. This impression was reinforced by her kangaroo-skin cowboy boots and her Texas twang. She stared down at us for a long stretch, her expression wavering between disappointment, disgust, and downright anger.

"Boys," she said at last, "I was wondering when I'd see you again."

My face went hot and I looked down at my sneakers. I always hated disappointing her, and yet somehow, when

Benny and I got together, I often did. Someday I'd have to take a look at that.

Ushering us into her office, Mrs. Johnson shut the door. We stood before her desk in the about-to-be-disciplined position. Without a word, our principal stalked all the way around us, lips drawn tight and eyes narrowed.

My imagination supplied all the painful ways she could punish us, from dipping us in boiling oil to feeding us to the crocodiles. I even checked the carpet for bloodstains, my mental images were that real.

At last, she rounded the desk and sank into her chair with a whisper of a sigh.

"A food fight? Really?"

Benny and I gave an apologetic shrug. It didn't sound like the kind of comment that needed a response.

"Are you deliberately trying to give me gray hair?"

Again we said nothing. We're not particularly wise, but it seemed the wise thing to do.

Our principal examined us with a gaze more powerful than the Hubble Telescope on steroids. "Has your cheese slid plumb off its cracker?" she asked. "What on earth possessed you to start a food fight?"

"Spring fever?" said Benny, working on an ingratiating smile.

"It's fall," said Mrs. Johnson.

"We've always been ahead of our time," I said.

She shook her head in that slow, serious way that lets you know you've nearly busted her disappointment meter. I examined the carpet again.

"Honestly, boys," said Mrs. Johnson, "if children are the future, I'm getting worried about it. I can't imagine why you'd do what you did."

Even Benny winced at that, but we couldn't very well tell her the real reason for the fight, could we? A hero doesn't go to the principal for help—to say nothing of the fact that she'd send us to a shrink if we tried.

"The truth is, we were, um, protesting," I said.

She frowned. "Protesting?" Benny looked confused.

"Yeah," I said, "protesting the, uh, separate food for boys and girls. It's not right."

"And it's not fair," Benny chimed in, catching up. "We demand equality."

Mrs. Johnson turned a skeptical gaze on us. "You've got a funny way of asking for it."

"Everyone should eat the same food," I said.

"Yeah," said Benny. "Why two separate meals all of a sudden?"

Steepling her fingers, Mrs. Johnson gave us the Principal Stare. As stares go, it was a good one, right up there with the Green Goblin Glare and the Cruella de Vil Sneer.

"Not that it's any of your business," she said, "but girls and boys have different nutritional requirements. So the cafeteria staff came up with this as a way to fine-tune our food delivery and save money."

I scratched my head. "Wait, you mean serving two different lunches every day is actually *cheaper*?"

"They have the expense reports to prove it," said our principal. "But we're getting off track. Since food fights are not a legitimate form of protest, we should be discussing your punishment."

"Torture us all you like," said Benny, getting into his role, "but you can never take away . . . our freedom!"

Mrs. Johnson lifted an eyebrow. I elbowed Benny. No use giving her any ideas.

"We don't believe in torture here at Monterrosa Elementary," said our principal. (Although anyone who'd experienced standardized testing might disagree.) "But we do believe in making the penalty fit the crime. Since the lunch ladies have refused to let you wash dishes, your punishment will be . . ."

I gritted my teeth, bracing myself.

"Helping Mr. Decker clean up the cafeteria, and two days of detention."

"Aw, but—" Benny began.

"Starting now," said Mrs. Johnson.

When he tried to protest again, I kicked Benny's ankle. It had just occurred to me that this particular punishment might actually work in our favor.

"We're really sorry, Mrs. Johnson," I said. "We'll go help Mr. Boo—um, Decker right away."

She scrubbed a hand over her face. "As if I didn't have enough to worry about with a student gone missing," she said, half to herself.

I perked up a little. Maybe there was a way we could learn something. . . .

"You mean Justin?" I said. "Has there been any sign of him?" It had been a full day, and I was worried about the kid.

Mrs. Johnson shook her head. "Vanished like the last slice of peach pie."

"Have you tried look—" Benny began.

"We've searched everywhere, thank you," she said. "I appreciate your concern, but you two have done enough for one day."

"Thanks," I said. "I mean, sorry?"

She squinted at us. "It'd make me happier than a gopher in soft dirt if I never had to call you into my office again."

"Us too," said Benny. "Believe me."

Mrs. Johnson made a shooing motion. "Now skedaddle!"

What else could we do? We skedaddled.

Chapter Nine

Taped Crusader

"**W**HY WERE YOU so eager to sign up for hard labor after we already picked up trash?" Benny asked as we trudged back to the cafeteria. "Do you *like* cruel and unusual punishment?"

"Well," I said, "I have voluntarily eaten your mom's vegan tofu snack balls."

He grimaced. "Don't remind me."

"But no, I was thinking of our investigation. The more time we spend in the cafeteria, the better chance we have of figuring this thing out."

"The sooner, the better," said Benny. "Who knows what those fake lunch ladies have got planned."

"Whatever it is," I said, "I'll bet it's not a pony ride in the park." I frowned. It struck me as odd that the cafeteria workers wouldn't let us wash dishes, the lowliest of kitchen tasks. Something was definitely up.

As if to underline this, on the way to the lunchroom, we saw some strange sights. A second-grade girl stealing a soccer ball from a pair of fourth-grade boys. Cheyenne and Gabi arm wrestling. And a pack of fifth-grade girls treeing a boy in their grade, then chucking old milk cartons at him.

It seemed like our Monterrosa females were taking girl power a bit too literally. In fact, even my own sister was acting stranger than a rhino dancing the rumba. When we bumped into her, I mentioned that we were still looking for her missing friend.

Her lips pursed. "Justin? He's not even a supporting player—more like a walk-on."

"Huh?"

"Who needs him?" snapped Veronica. "He's a booger face." And she flounced away.

This from the girl who'd begged me to find her friend.

But girl-related strangeness was another mystery for another day. As ordered, Benny and I reported to Mr. Boo, who was scouring tomato sauce off the cafeteria walls.

"Dudes," he said, wagging his head, "I can't believe you started a food fight."

"Yeah, well . . ." I shrugged uncomfortably.

"On the one hand, it's awesome," said the grizzled surfer. "But on the other, it's a ton of work for whoever has to clean it up." A sudden smile lit his face as he tossed us two sponges. "Luckily, that someone is you."

Mr. Boo kept scrubbing at the high stuff we couldn't reach, and assigned us everything from his waist level down. Dunking my sponge into the pail of soapy water, I surveyed the aftereffects of our food fight. With all the puddles of lasagna, Jell-O, succotash, and gravy, the place looked like a family of rabid wolverines had dismantled an Italian Thanksgiving.

As Benny and I swept and swabbed and scrubbed, I kept an eye on the kitchen. The lunch ladies had lowered the serving-counter grille, but left the kitchen door half-way open. Various thumps and clatters came from behind it, along with occasional bursts of clickety-clacks.

Ever so casually, Benny and I headed over to tidy up the part of the lunchroom that gave us the best view of the kitchen.

"See anything?" Benny asked.

I swept up some stray pasta and sneaked a look. "Mrs. Robinson is . . . arguing with Mrs. McCoy."

The click-clacking escalated as they waved their hands wildly, getting up in each other's face. Mrs. Perez stepped between them.

"What are they saying?" Benny asked.

I edged closer. "Beats me. Sounds like a dolphin concert."

As I watched, Mrs. Robinson threw off Mrs. Perez's restraining hand, spun, and punched the jumbo-size refrigerator with a mighty blow. I gasped.

"Now she's beating up the fridge," I said. Even from here, I could spot the enormous dent. Mrs. Robinson was unharmed. "And she's winning."

"No human could do that, not even Batman. What could they be?" Benny straightened from mopping up a gravy lake and craned his neck to see. "Ooh, what if these freaks are *wearing* the real lunch ladies, like a costume?"

"First, eeww," I said. "And second, I don't think that's possible."

He gave me an ominous look. "If they're aliens," he said, "we have no idea *what's* possible."

Benny had a point. I brushed a pile of random food bits into the dustpan as Mrs. Perez slammed the kitchen door with a suspicious glare, cutting off our view. "If only there was some way for us to get a good look around in there. Who knows what we might find?"

A crafty expression spread over Benny's normally innocent features, like a pat of butter on a hot tortilla. He cast a sidelong glance at the custodian's cart, which stood near the wall, not far away.

"Correct me if I'm wrong," he muttered, "but doesn't the head janitor have keys to all the doors at school?"

"You're right, but you're wrong," I said. "We are *not* going to steal Mr. Boo's keys."

"Borrow," Benny corrected me.

Shaking my head, I said, "Not even." I glanced over at

the lanky custodian, who was cleaning up across the room, whistling away. "(a), he would totally notice in five minutes flat. And (b), we could get suspended."

"Spoilsport," said Benny, pouting.

"There's got to be a better way," I mused, studying the cart. And then my gaze landed on the invention no guy can do without. Duct tape. Checking out the kitchen door, I noticed it had no dead bolt, just the single lock in the knob. *Hmm* . . .

I carried the full dustpan over to a garbage can, not far from Mr. Boo. Jerking my head at the kitchen, I asked, "How late do they stay around?"

"The lunch ladies?" he said. "Maybe another half hour. They split long before second recess."

"Do they lock up when they go, or do you?"

"Sometimes they do," he said, "but mostly it's me. Why do you ask?"

Tipping the contents of my dustpan into the trash, I thought fast. "Um, I was thinking about being a custodian when I grow up. Just wanted to know what it involves."

That was both the right and the wrong thing to say. It did distract Mr. Boo from wondering about my motives, but it also set him off on a five-minute monologue about how totally awesome it was to be a custodian.

The class bell rang, and Benny and I had to go.

"Later, dudes!" Mr. Boo waved as we left. "Come help

anytime." Then something on the floor caught his eye, so he stooped, picked it up, and showed us a small green vegetable. "Hey. Whisper words of wisdom, lima bean."

"Uh, right." Custodians say the darnedest things. I smiled and waved as we left, but I felt a little bad about having borrowed his roll of duct tape.

I felt even worse about slipping a piece of it over the lock mechanism in the outer cafeteria door. But all heroes have to bend the rules sometimes. It's practically in the hero handbook.

Or if it isn't, it should be.

Turned out, the hardest part of my plan was sneaking back into the cafeteria to rig the kitchen door after the lunch ladies had left but before Mr. Boo locked it. What excuse to use? Returning books to the library? Mr. Chu told me to wait until after school. Talking to the principal? Ditto.

I couldn't just make a break for it. Mr. Chu was pretty mellow, but even he tended to frown on kids wandering off during class time. We were halfway through our design-your-own-dinosaur unit when it suddenly struck me.

I was overthinking. When in doubt, turn to the classics. I raised my hand. "Mr. Chu, can I go to the bathroom?"

Benny shot a glance my way.

"Are you physically able to go to the bathroom?" said our teacher. "I'm guessing the answer is yes, or you wouldn't still be alive. But if you're asking for permission to go right now, the answer is . . ." He paused dramatically. "Yes. Go!"

I left walking like a guy who has to use the restroom, but as soon as I was out of sight, I sprinted for the cafeteria.

Tearing past the third-grade rooms, I heard the drone of kids reciting their times tables. Out beyond the buildings, the playground was as deserted as an all-you-can-eat menudo buffet. Luck was with me.

Hustling down the hallway, I stopped only when I reached the door I'd taped earlier. It swung open on a darkened cafeteria.

So far, so good.

The empty room still smelled of tomato sauce and gravy, the aftermath of our food fight. With the duct tape bulging in my pocket, I crossed to the kitchen door and tried it. Closed but not locked.

I pulled out a short strip of the tape and tore it with my teeth—*scritchhh!*

And a woman's voice said, "What the H-E-double-toothpicks are you doing in here?"

Chapter Ten

Chicken Snoop

I **WHIRLED.** In the dimness before me stood the familiar figure of Mrs. Ponytail, the PTA mom. She looked just as surprised to see me as I was to see her.

"What are you doing?" she demanded again.

"I, uh, what?" I said. Because I'm so good with words. Casually, I tried to hide the duct tape behind my back.

"You shouldn't be here." She scowled. "Why aren't you in class, bothering your teacher and pretending to learn something?" Mrs. Ponytail advanced, and although she was still the same PTA mom as before, an uneasy tickle, like the feet of many daddy longlegs, crept across my flesh.

"I'm uh, doing something for my, um, teacher," I said.

Mrs. Ponytail loomed over me. Her flowery perfume was so strong it could have beaten up Iron Man and Spider-Man without even breaking a sweat. Her voice grew lower, rougher. "I know all about boys like you. Trouble-makers and promise-breakers, yes indeed. Boys that lie and steal."

Are you talking about an old boyfriend or your son? I thought. But what I said was, "Honestly, I was just—" I gestured with one hand, still keeping the hand with the tape behind me.

"Helping yourself to free food, like a looter and pillager?" said Mrs. Ponytail. "Go ahead. Tell me another—"

"Ah, *there* you are!" Sunlight speared into the murky room, outlining Benny's silhouette in the doorway. "Mr. Chu was wondering."

The PTA mom whirled to confront Benny. I took advantage of the distraction to fumble behind me for the doorknob.

"And why in the name of all that's wholesome are *you* here?" Mrs. Ponytail demanded of Benny.

I motioned at him to stretch out his explanation.

"Here on this earth, here at school, or here in the caf-eteria?" he said. "I'm only here in school because the law makes me. But why I'm here on this planet is complex and mysterious—something I may not be able to figure out until I've lived most of my life."

You've got to hand it to Benny—he can do annoying and thickheaded better than almost anyone. His little speech gave me the time I needed. I opened the door, covered the latch with duct tape, pushed the button on the inside knob, and spun back around, closing the door behind me.

If Mrs. Ponytail were a cartoon, she'd have had little frustration lines bursting out of her head. Benny has that effect sometimes. She ground her teeth and practically growled, "Unless you want that life cut tragically short, you'll leave now."

I raised my hands in surrender. "Sure thing," I said. "We were just going. Weren't we, Benny?"

"Yup, yup," he said. "Lots of learning left in the day. I can't wait to fill my head with fascinating factoids."

We nodded pleasantly to the PTA mom, who was practically pulling off her ponytail, and strolled out the door.

"Did Mr. Chu really send you?" I asked Benny as we hustled back to class.

He snorted. "Same as you, I asked to go to the bathroom. Is the tape in place?"

"All set," I said. "Everything's ready for Operation Kitchen Snoop."

Before that, of course, there were lessons to get through, detention to serve, and what was left of the afternoon to kill. But Benny and I are nothing if not resourceful. Finally, as the sun sank low, we made an excuse to my mom, promised we'd be home for dinner, and rode our bikes back to Monterrosa Elementary.

There's something almost sad about a school with

nobody in it. The flagpole stood as bare as a Q-tip. No kids shouted on the playground. No cars graced the parking lot.

We were alone.

After stashing our bikes in some nearby bushes, we made our way to the outer cafeteria door. Amazingly, the tape still covered the latch. Mr. Boo must have been too into his after-school surfing safari to double-check whether everything was locked up.

Sometimes, you get lucky.

The door creaked open, and we slipped inside. Darkness pooled in the corners as the last sunlight bled away from the room.

Benny reached for the wall switch.

I stopped him. "Don't. The light will show through the windows."

"Okay, then," he said, "break out the flashlight."

"I thought you were going to bring it."

"I thought *you* had it," he said.

Pointing at the lump in the pocket of his hoodie, I asked, "Then what's that?"

Benny reached in and drew out a spray can of Raid insecticide. "Insurance," he said. "In case things get seriously buggy."

I wiped my palms on my jeans, surprised to discover that they were sweaty. The thought of running into an alien or an enormous insect had me feeling a bit jumpy. Benny caught my reaction.

"Chill," he said. "Nobody's here. No cars in the lot."

"Maybe that's because alien bug monsters don't drive," I said.

Benny's smile looked a little less confident. "Heh," he said. "Good one."

We crossed the cafeteria to the kitchen. Here too my tape had stayed in place—the door swung open without a sound. I felt a swell of confidence.

Too bad we weren't master criminals; school security was pretty laid-back.

As soon as we stepped inside, though, second thoughts ambushed me.

"Maybe this wasn't such a hot idea," I said. "What if they sleep here or something?"

Benny scoffed. "You're thinking of vampires."

My pulse throbbed in my temples. "For all we know, they could be some kind of vampire E.T.s."

"Relax," said Benny. "You worry too much."

"And you don't worry enough."

The last weak rays of sunshine struggled to penetrate the high, filthy window above the sink. They mostly failed. Vague shapes loomed in the dimness—the refrigerator here, the food-prep island there. The ghostly aromas of burritos, pizza, and so many school meals haunted the room.

It was just a kitchen. But somehow the place seemed different after hours.

Spookier.

More sinister.

"Hello?" Benny called. "Anybody home?"

I shushed him. "If someone *is* here," I whispered, "we don't want them to hear us."

We listened intently. But all we heard was the soft whir of the jumbo-size refrigerator and the faint gurgle of water in the pipes.

"See? We're alone," said Benny, plunging on ahead into the dimness.

"So what are we looking for?" I said.

Biting his lip, Benny scanned the space. "Anything that seems out of place. Alien technology, giant egg sacs, kidnapped boys, a lunch that actually tastes good . . ."

"That narrows it down," I said.

He pulled open some cabinets under the counter and peeked inside.

"Um, a bit small for a missing kid," I said.

"Not if he was chopped up," said Benny.

I grimaced. "Morbid much?"

With that cheerful thought in mind, I peeked into the space under the sink. Nothing there but the dim shapes of pipes and cleaning products. The harsh tang of ammonia cut through the funk of old hot dogs and fryer grease.

The deeper we moved into the kitchen, the more I had the sensation of being watched. Twice I spun around, ninja fast. And twice I spotted nothing but cabinets, a deep fryer, and the usual kitchen junk.

"You sure we're alone?" I asked Benny.

He paused with his hand on the pull bar of the fridge. "Sure. Why?"

"I keep getting this 'spiders up the back' feeling."

Benny smirked. "Try changing your shirt every week or so."

"Oh, ha ha," I said. "Your wit's so bright, who needs a flashlight?"

"And speaking of light . . ." Benny opened the fridge and its bulb shone forth, casting even darker shadows into the corners of the room.

"Kind of big for a flashlight, but it works," I said.

Benny poked his head into the fridge and began rummaging around.

"Seriously?" I said.

"Hey, you never know. Might be some pudding in need of rescue."

I wagged my head. "The sacrifices you make for your school . . ."

"Inspiring, isn't it?" said Benny.

As he searched for a snack, I headed into the shadowy corner to investigate a mysterious door—the pantry, maybe?—that I could just make out. Beside it, some brooms and what might have been a rolled-up rug leaned against the wall.

I tried the door. Locked tight.

Fumbling in my pocket for the skeleton key I'd gotten from a comic-book coupon and always wanted to try, I dropped the danged thing. As it turned out, clumsiness saved my life.

I squatted to grab the key.

The shadows stirred.

And then a thick something-or-other whooshed just above my head, impaling itself in the door with a *thunk*.

Chapter Eleven

All About
the Chase

I LOOKED UP. Above me, I made out a tall, many-limbed form with a triangular head. One of those limbs had nearly speared me like a shish kebab. Now it was stuck in the pantry door, and the creature was tugging to release it.

"Yaaah!" I cried. Rolling away from the spooky whatchamacallit, I sprang to my feet.

As I sprinted out of the corner, Benny's pale face poked around the fridge door. He gripped the can of Raid in his hand.

"What is it?" he asked.

"There's something back there," I said, "and it really hates visitors."

The rest of what happened next you already know—how

we ran screaming, how Benny blasted the Raid all over the kitchen on the way out, and how we were chased by a six-foot-tall insect creature wearing an apron.

What you don't know is how we got out of that pickle.

Benny and I reached the kitchen door a few feet ahead of the monster, and it hissed with rage. We blasted through, slammed the door behind us, and kept running.

The door hit the creature with a *thud*.

Glancing back, I saw the panel blow open again.

"Gah!" I gasped. "The door didn't stop it."

"No duh," said Benny. "You taped over the lock."

The bug monster emitted a blistering stream of clicks, rubbed its sore nose, and took off after us. I assumed we'd just been cursed out in insect-ese.

Hotfooting it across the cafeteria, Benny and I made straight for the exit. I checked behind us again.

"It's gaining!" I cried.

A tall gray trash can stood near the door. Benny, a little ahead of me, grabbed the empty container, whirled, and bowled it toward the monster.

"*Nnargh!*" it shouted, in a garbled insect-human voice.

The creature jumped to clear the can, but not soon enough.

Tchoom! Its legs (the lower two, anyway) were swept out from beneath it, and the huge insect went down hard.

His eyes wide and wild, Benny sprayed the Raid in a wide swath at our pursuer. "Take that, you six-legged freak!"

All it did was make me cough.

"Come—*back*—on!" I yelled, grabbing his arm.

We hit the exit door's push bar and blasted out into the cool evening. I don't think I've ever run that fast—not even when Randy Sparks mistakenly came after me for supergluing his desk shut. (It was actually Benny who did the deed.)

Hurtling across the blacktop, we made for the bushes where we'd hidden our bikes. The giant insect kicked open the door, clicking like a castanet festival. As I watched, two sets of translucent extensions unfurled from its back.

A full-body shudder rippled through me at the sight.

"Not fair!" I cried.

"What?" said Benny, not slowing down.

"It's got wings!"

Benny glanced over his shoulder and his eyes got huge. "Gaah!" he yelled. "I hate nature!"

The monster beat its wings and lifted into the air.

"Here it comes!" I panted. My imagination ran wild with images of the creature catching us, biting our heads off, and slurping down our insides like one of those wax-bottle candies you get for Halloween.

For once, my imagination may not have been exaggerating.

We plowed into the bushes, grabbed our bikes, and hopped onto them. The monster followed, touching down on the ground every five or ten feet. I guessed that its wings couldn't carry it for very long. By now the sun had set, and the school's amber security lights winked on, turning the creature the yellowish green of fresh snot.

Its eyes were huge, soulless, and hungry.

Benny and I pumped our pedals for all we were worth, speeding across the blacktop. I was never so grateful for wheels in all my life. Gradually—not soon enough for me—the monster fell behind. By the time we reached the road outside the school, the creature had given up. With a last faint cry of *"Kreeaugh!"* it wheeled and headed back to the cafeteria.

Still, Benny and I didn't slow down until we were halfway home. Side by side, we jetted down the street past late afternoon joggers, parents returning from work, and a handful of kids still out playing in their driveways.

Everything looked so normal. And yet we knew this town was anything but.

My heartbeat gradually slowed from speed-metal to something like classic-rock tempo. But my brain was still as jumbled as a bowlful of taco stew.

"¡Ay no!" I gasped.

"You said it," said Benny. His face was whiter than a polar bear's ghost.

"Th-that," I stuttered. "That thing?"

"I know, right?" he said. "Dang."

I sucked in a deep breath. "What is it with Monterrosa and monsters?"

"Beats me," said Benny. "But you'd think, after we'd tackled were-hyenas, that a giant bug would be no big deal."

"But you'd be wrong." I shivered.

The last of the twilight was fading, swallowed by the night. We cycled onward.

"I mean, how is that even possible?" I asked. "A six-foot insect?"

"How is it possible that they canceled *Commando Nanny* before even airing an episode?" said Benny. "Some things just are."

I cocked my head, considering. "True."

"The real question is: What are we going to do about it?"

We pedaled in silence for half a block, thinking it over.

"We could try to find their spaceship," I said, "assuming they're aliens."

"And then destroy it?" said Benny. "Might work, or might just make 'em madder."

"But what if that thing's not an alien?" I said.

"Uh . . ." Benny scrunched up his face in thought. "We call an exterminator?"

"Yeah," I said, "because your can of Raid worked so well. Maybe we should just go ahead and tell someone, like Mrs. Johnson, or our parents?"

"Are you kidding?" Benny scowled. "Whatever happened to being a hero? Whatever happened to toughing it out, because that's what heroes do?"

"Well, I—"

"Do heroes run to mommy and daddy every time things get a little scary?"

"Uh, no," I admitted.

"So are we heroes or are we wusses?" Benny said.

I lifted a shoulder. "Is wussy hero one of the choices?" But I knew he had me—we would see this thing through, no matter what.

He swerved to avoid a pothole in the road. "Problem is, we don't know enough about this kind of insect."

"We could look it up," I said.

"Nope, we need more—the inside scoop. We need to talk to a bug guy, pronto."

"I think they're called entomologists," I said.

"Woo, check out the big brain on Carlos," said Benny.

I spared a hand to polish my knuckles on my chest. "Extra-credit vocabulary word," I said. But the gesture was as hollow as a drum. I was still shaken.

"So where do we find this . . . entomologist?" asked Benny as we turned onto my street.

"I dunno," I said. "But I know a guy who might."

"Who's that?"

Pulling to a stop in my driveway, I smiled. "Our old friend Mr. Google."

Chapter Twelve

Last Janitor Standing

ALL THINGS CONSIDERED, Benny and I decided to brown-bag it the next day. Never mind that the bizarro lunch ladies might be spiking our food; it just didn't seem sanitary to have your lunch prepared by giant bugs. (I tried to convince Veronica to follow our example, but she just chucked a carrot at me.)

Also, I realized that if that monster had recognized us last night, we might not get the warmest reception at the cafeteria.

Now we had twin problems: one, staying out of the lunch ladies' clutches, and two, stopping whatever evil buggy plans they had cooked up for our school.

So, no pressure.

Our Internet search the night before hadn't turned up

much in the way of local insect experts. No surprise there. Our town's not that big. When we asked my mom and grandma about it, Abuelita said she knew an entomologist at the natural history museum with the unlikely name of Dr. Memphis Sincere.

But since we couldn't see him until after we'd served detention, Benny and I decided to make the best use of our time before school. (And speaking of detention, I kinda sorta forgot to mention it to my parents. I considered it a public service to them—they had enough on their minds.)

First, we woke up ugly-early and rode our bikes to the neighborhood around Monterrosa Elementary. While other kids were still yawning and brushing their teeth, we wheeled through alleyways and vacant lots, searching for any place you could stow a spaceship.

The whole time, I was jumpier than a froghopper on a hot rock. I *really* didn't want to stumble across that giant bug again, but you can't be a hero without going through some scary stuff.

The fields were empty of flying saucers. And unless the spaceship was disguised as a trash bin, the alleys were too. We briefly considered the town water tower, but since the tank had been there forever and didn't look particularly flight-worthy, we abandoned it. I secretly breathed a sigh of relief. Running into monsters so early in the morning can put a crimp in your whole day.

Arriving well before school would start, Benny and

I locked up our bikes. A light burned in the front office, but the rest of the buildings lay dark, deserted. When we headed over to the cafeteria, another light shone through the filthy kitchen window, and the faint clatter of pots and pans reached us.

The lunch ladies had beaten us there.

"Man, I'd really like to get a look inside that pantry," I said. "What if they're stashing Veronica's friend in there?"

"Little Jethro?" said Benny.

"Justin," I said. "His parents called my dad last night, asking if he was staying over with Veronica. He's still missing."

"You don't think they . . . ?" Benny brought his hand to his mouth in an eating gesture.

"His parents ate him?"

Benny rolled his eyes. "No, dummy. But maybe the lunch ladies did."

Wow. It hadn't hit me until that moment, but given what we'd seen last night, I could now believe they were the kind of insects that might eat a second grader.

"Maybe . . ." I said, feeling queasy. I paced. "I sure hope not. Is there anything else three giant bugs might want with a little kid?"

"Staging a remake of 'Goldilocks and the Three Bears'?" When I frowned, Benny held up a hand. "Bad joke. Hey, but I bet I know someone who could get us into the pantry."

Hope quickened my heart. "You mean . . . ?"

"The one and only Mr. Boo."

And that's how we found ourselves outside the boys' bathroom with a shaggy janitor before the start of school. Mr. Boo's cart in the hall had tipped us off to his location, and we discovered him mopping ferociously at a black spot on the floor.

"Geez, think you dudes could try spitting out your gum in a trash can sometimes?" he said.

I winced. "On behalf of all fourth-grade boys, I apologize."

Mr. Boo nodded. "Apology accepted. What's shakin', amigos?"

"It's about the cafeteria kitchen," I began.

"Have you ever been inside the pantry?" said Benny.

The custodian leaned on his mop handle and scratched his head. "Me, personally? No."

"If there was something funny going on in there, could you get in?" I asked.

One corner of his mouth quirked up. "Something funny? Are the lunch ladies serving clown fish?"

I offered a polite smile at his feeble joke, and glanced at Benny. How much should we tell him? I wondered. We needed the custodian as an ally, and for some reason, I thought that raving about giant bugs might drive him away.

"You heard about that missing boy?" I asked.

"Which one?" said the custodian.

"What do you mean?" Benny stiffened.

Mr. Boo waved his hand in a *poof* gesture. "Two boys have gone missing: Justin Delgado and Nathan Sakamoto. We searched all over school for them."

Benny gnawed his lip.

A sour taste filled my mouth. *Two* kids gone? This was getting out of hand.

"Um, did you search the pantry?" I asked.

The janitor frowned. "No, just the kitchen. Why? You think they might be in there?"

"I'd check it out," said Benny. "They could have wandered in when the lunch ladies weren't looking, then gotten locked inside."

"And they didn't think to pound on the door?" said the custodian.

I could tell Mr. Boo wasn't convinced yet. "You know how little kids are," I said. "They probably cried themselves to sleep."

Or the lunch ladies gagged them.

Or ate them.

The custodian nodded. At least he was considering it.

"On a completely different topic," Benny said, "got any mega-jumbo-size cans of Raid?"

Chapter Thirteen

Judy Rude-y

MUCH LIKE A patient in a dentist's waiting room, the school day simmered with anxiety. And it wasn't helped by the discovery that AJ was absent and no one knew why. Was he just sick? Or had something happened to him?

Something bug-related?

At lunch, Benny and I cautiously patrolled the lunchroom, even though we'd brown-bagged it. Today, Mrs. Perez was supervising the serving area. When we entered, her dark eyes locked onto us like heat-seeking missiles.

"See that?" Benny muttered.

"Mm-hm," I said. Although I knew she wouldn't try anything with so many witnesses, my stomach flip-flopped like a circus acrobat.

We walked deeper into the cafeteria, and the lunch lady's gaze tracked us, unblinking. As if she'd been summoned,

Mrs. Robinson emerged from the kitchen. She too stopped and stared. I wouldn't swear to it, but it seemed like their heads swiveled farther to keep us in sight than a human head could swivel.

Tearing my eyes away from the creepy cooks, I scoped out the lunchroom. At first glance, it looked the same as before, including separate meals for boys and girls. Then Benny spotted something.

"Check out the girls," he said.

"What about them?" I asked.

And then I saw it. At table after table, the girls were the noisiest, rowdiest, and most active. I saw Gabi Acosta give a boy a wedgie, Cheyenne Summers steal José's dessert, and Tina Green put some guy in a headlock.

"Look at how they're acting," said Benny. "Loud, rude, and obnoxious. They're acting—"

"Like us," I said. "Like boys."

It was true. Usually, most girls at our school fell into the "Why can't you be more like her?" category. But today, they could have been residents of the monkey cage at the zoo.

"Why aren't the lunch monitors doing anything?" Benny wondered aloud.

Scanning the room for their blue vests, I soon saw why. "They're all girls," I said. "AJ's gone, and I don't know what happened to the other boy."

We were so busy checking out the scene, Benny and I nearly bumped into one of them.

"You two," said the girl, a tall fifth grader with thick, braided pigtails like Pippi Longstocking. "Why are you here?"

"We came to use the Jacuzzi," said Benny. "Obviously."

Her face darkened. Not a big fan of sarcasm. I noticed her laminated name tag read TENACITY. "We're in the cafeteria," she said. "There's no Jacuzzi here."

Benny lifted a shoulder. "I was misinformed."

Tenacity's fists landed on her narrow hips. "Okay, buster. Get lost."

Holding up my bag, I said, "We just want to eat our lunch."

Her hands shot out, surprisingly strong, and gripped our upper arms. Spinning us toward the door and hustling us along, Tenacity said, "Take your pitiful peanut-butter sandwiches outside."

Benny shrugged her off. "It's a lunchroom," he said. "We can eat wherever we want."

"Not on my watch," she growled. "No brown-baggers. Especially not boys."

Then the lunch monitor shot out both hands and shoved Benny's chest. Backward he staggered, until he stumbled and fell.

"Hey, you can't treat my friend like that!" I cried, my body tensing.

"Watch me," she snapped. Grabbing my arm, Tenacity slung me after him. I couldn't help it; I tripped over Benny.

Applause and hoots came from the girls at the nearest table. "So graceful!" one of them called. "You should be on *Stumbling with the Stars*!"

My blush smoldered like a bad sunburn, and I couldn't help clenching my fists as we got up. But as every boy knows, you're not supposed to hit a girl. Especially if she's bigger than you.

"Maybe we *will* eat outside," said Benny. "It stinks in here."

Tenacity snarled and took a step closer, and two fifth-grade girls at the table stood up beside her, glowering.

"You haven't heard the last of this." I edged backward. "We'll tell Principal Johnson about you."

"Go ahead," said Tenacity. "She'll probably cheer."

At that comment, my throat went tight. Mrs. Johnson was female—would she turn anti-boy too?

Benny and I retreated at a slow amble so anyone watching would know we weren't scared. Somehow I don't think the girls at the nearest table got the message; they ushered us out with chickenlike *bwak bwak*s.

"Okay, that was weird," I said.

"Girls are weird," said Benny.

We found a seat at one of the outside benches. "Not that kind of weird. Do you think the way they're acting is connected with the lunch ladies?"

Unwrapping his lunch, Benny said, "You mean, like they took Mrs. Robinson's girl-power rant too seriously?"

I bit into my peanut-butter-and-jelly sandwich. "Every single girl in the lunchroom? No, I think it's more than that."

"Some kind of alien mind ray?"

"Maybe. Or maybe the lunch ladies are putting something in the girls' food to make them wacko. Maybe that's why they're giving us separate meals."

Benny stared dubiously at his collard-green wrap with hummus and veggies. "Well, they say you are what you eat."

"If that's the case, you should be a block of tofu by now." I smirked.

"Trade you half?" he asked, holding up part of his wrap.

I sighed and swapped him for my tortilla chips, because that's what friends do.

"But why would the lunch ladies be doing this?" I said. "And what could they be putting in the lunches to turn the girls so *loco*?"

"Chili peppers? Bug juice?"

We had no answers, so we concentrated on what we did have: food. In no time, we'd finished up our lunch (except for the collard-green wrap) and dumped our trash in the bin. By now, kids were leaving the cafeteria, and I spotted someone who might have some answers.

"Let's go ask Tina," I said.

Our classmate was pretty cool for a girl—heck, for anybody. She practiced karate moves, had a great collection of comic books, and was tough to scare. She'd stood beside us against the were-hyenas, and had become a real friend. As a certified girl, she was in an excellent position to help us now.

Tina swaggered out the door with Gabi and a skinny red-haired girl I didn't know on either side. All were cackling at some joke.

"Hey, Tina," I said. "Gabi."

Tina turned to the redhead. "Do you smell something?"

"Smells like a massive influx of cooties." Skinny Red sniffed.

Pretending to spot us for the first time, Tina said, "Well, if it isn't the two kings of boy cooties, Brackman and Rivera."

I frowned. This wasn't like her at all.

"*We've* got cooties?" said Benny. "Girls are the ones!"

Before they could get into some kind of major fight, I jumped in. "Tina, could we talk to you? It's important."

She rolled her eyes. "Oh, I'm sure."

"You don't need to go with them," said Skinny Red. "Boys are inferior."

I held up a hand to Benny before he could retort. "Please?" I said.

Tina patted her friend's arm. "Don't worry, I can handle these two nerds without even breaking a sweat." She sauntered away from the girls to join us on the side. "What?"

"There's something strange going on with the lunch ladies," I said.

"So?" She crossed her arms.

Benny gave her a funny look. "Is this the same girl who couldn't wait to solve the whole were-hyena mystery?"

She snorted. "That was so last month."

"We think the lunch ladies are feeding you girls something weird to change you," I said.

Tina laughed. "What they're feeding us is better food than you guys get. You're jealous."

"You're nuts," said Benny.

My gut twisted. Something was very wrong here.

"And they've really opened my eyes on this whole girl-power thing," Tina said. "The lunch ladies rock!"

Heat rose through my chest like a chili-pepper burn. "They're giant bugs in disguise, and they're only using you for their evil purposes!"

Overhearing this, Gabi and Skinny Red giggled.

Tina examined me like I was something questionable she'd found on the sole of her shoe. "You are deeply whacked, Rivera. Mrs. McCoy was right—boys are jerks, losers, and a total waste of space."

The calmer she got, the more out of control I felt. "You're the jerk!" I cried.

"Oh, please." Tina glanced back at her posse and circled her index finger around her ear in the universal sign for *he's cracked*. They snickered.

But I couldn't stop. "What's wrong with you? You know

there's weird stuff out there—you've seen it. And I'm telling you the lunch ladies are *not human*."

"He's right," said Benny. "We've seen it for ourselves."

"Then you're both looney tunes," Tina sneered. She flapped the back of her hand at us in a brushing-off gesture and turned to go.

I felt raw inside, like someone had scraped sixty-grit sandpaper over my innards. "What's up with you?" I repeated. "I thought we were friends."

At this, Tina glanced back over her shoulder, wide-eyed. Was I finally getting through to her?

"Haw, haw, haw!" She burst out in a belly laugh.

Apparently not.

As Tina rejoined her crew, Benny caught my shoulder and steered me away. "Ignore her. Like I said, Carlos—girls are weird."

But my eyes prickled and my stomach felt like a milk carton someone had stomped on. Not only were the mutant-insect lunch ladies threatening my school, they were taking away my friends.

And that I would not stand for.

My jaw clenched. These bugs were going down.

Chapter Fourteen

Bugging Out with the Bug Doctor

A**S SOON AS** the Detention Queen, Ms. Pebblecreek, released us from our after-school punishment, Benny and I shot from the room like a loogie from a lip. Collecting our bikes, we made straight for the Monterrosa Natural History Museum and our town's biggest expert on insects.

At the end of Durfee Road squatted the museum, a low, wide building that smelled faintly of cheese. This time of day, only a handful of tourists wandered through its exhibits admiring the dioramas of sea animals, geological cross sections, and central Californian critters.

A bored-looking young woman with purple-streaked

hair and a shoulder tattoo of one of the X-Men sat at the front desk, texting away on her phone. She glanced up, mildly surprised that she had visitors.

"Go on in," said Purple Hair, popping her gum. "Kids under twelve are free."

"We're not into dioramas," said Benny, even though I knew he was.

"We're here to see Mr. Sincere," I said.

Purple Hair looked us up and down through her cool-girl glasses. "Aren't you kinda young to be scientists?"

"He'll want to see us," I said. "It's about giant bugs."

"Imagine my excitement," she said, all deadpan. "Second floor, room 202." Making a vague gesture toward the elevator, Purple Hair resumed texting.

"Wolverine is one of my favorite X-Men too," I said, pointing at her tattoo.

Her lip curled and she blew out a dismissive puff of air. "That's not Wolverine, that's Papa Smurf. Get a clue."

I apologized, although personally, I thought her tattoo artist could've used some art lessons.

Room 202 lay halfway down a dingy hall of offices that smelled like burned coffee and moldy carpet. The door hung open, but we rapped on it anyway.

"Mr. Sincere?" Benny called.

The room was a mess. Worse than my bedroom.

Stacks of scientific journals leaned against a battered, gunmetal-gray desk. Packed bookshelves filled one wall.

The rest of the space was jammed with cameras, microscopes, butterfly nets, a display case bristling with more kinds of beetles than there were TV channels, and loads and loads of framed and mounted moths and spiders.

I shuddered at the spiders. "Hello?"

A tight salt-and-pepper Afro peeked up from behind the desk. A long tea-colored face followed it. "Eh, how's that?" said the man.

"Are you Mr. Sincere?" I asked.

An enormous hazel eye blinked at us through one of those massive magnifying glasses scientists strap to their heads. A chill tickled the tops of my shoulders. What kind of man was this?

"That's *Doctor* Sincere," he huffed. "I didn't spend all that money on a PhD to be called mister."

"Doctor, we need your help," I said.

Dr. Sincere rose to his feet, blinking. His body was long and lanky with a potbelly, and draped in a tan jacket with lots of pockets, like hunters wear. He looked like a librarian on safari. The scientist dropped some small wriggly thing into a coffee can with his long tweezers.

"Mind the scorpions," he said.

"Scorpions?!"

Benny and I shuffled back a couple of steps, eyeing the carpet around us. Something scuttled from behind a stack of magazines and along the front of the desk. We both jumped.

"There's one!" I cried.

Surprisingly quick for an old guy, the scientist scooted around his desk and snagged the creature. I kept careful watch for others.

"So," said Dr. Sincere, "what did you want to see me about?"

"Er, uh," I said. Like I said, I'm good with words.

"Our school has been taken over by bugs," said Benny.

"If you've got cockroaches, call the exterminator," the scientist drawled, removing his magnifier headband. "That's not my department."

"You don't understand." I took a deep breath. "These are huge bugs, tall as you."

"And they're masquerading as our lunch ladies," said Benny.

At that, Dr. Sincere's eyes widened and his face went chalky. He groped blindly for the back of his chair and sank into his seat. "No," he breathed. "It's not possible."

"What isn't?" I asked.

This set off a flurry of blinks, like his eyeballs were sending an SOS. "What—what kind of insects did you say?"

"Tall, maybe six feet, and green," I said.

"With a triangular head and six legs," said Benny.

"And wings," I said. "Really gross-looking wings."

The scientist's face tightened. "Two sets of them?"

"Yeah," said Benny. "What kind of bug is it?"

Staring blindly at a spot on the wall, Dr. Sincere dropped his tweezers on the desk. He muttered, "Oh, no, no, no," over and over.

"I've never heard of that type before," Benny said.

I stepped closer. "Just tell us what they are and how to get rid of them."

A scorpion scurried from almost under my feet. *Yikes.* I made a noise like a mouse choking on a jalapeño, and hopped backward. The arachnid climbed onto a camera not three feet away from Dr. Sincere.

"There's another one!" said Benny.

But the scientist didn't move. He just kept repeating

himself, like a loop on a bad hip-hop track. Distracted, I glanced around his office for more critters on the loose. Benny took the tweezers, captured the scorpion, and dropped it into the coffee can.

A close-up photo on the wall caught my eye. Stepping closer, I peered at the big green bug with the folded forelegs.

"That's it, that's the one!" I said, reading the caption. *"Mantis religiosa."*

"Mantis?" said Benny. "Like praying mantis?"

We turned to the scientist. "What's going on here?" I said. "Why is that photo on your wall?"

Dr. Sincere sank his face into his hands. "I'm an entomologist," he mumbled. "I have oodles of insect photos."

Leaning on the man's desk, Benny said, "Yeah, but this insect got huge and is roaming around our school dishing up weirdness. What gives?"

A hazel eye peeked through a net of fingers. "I don't want to talk about it," said Dr. Sincere. "Go away."

"But we helped you catch the scorpions," said Benny.

"Leave me alone."

Anger bubbled up in me like some carbonated lava drink. "You know something!"

"No," he said.

"You do! These creatures are bad news. They're making kids disappear; they're turning my friends into jerks." I turned to Benny. "Not you, Benny."

"Of course not," he said.

I waved my pointer finger in the scientist's face. "You better tell us what's going on!"

"I can't, I can't," he moaned, covering his eyes again.

Benny and I stared at each other, stumped. It's kind of hard for a kid to force an unrelated grown-up to do anything. But then I remembered where we'd gotten the man's name.

"Abuelita," I said.

"You think she might . . . ?" Benny asked.

Fishing my cell phone from a pocket, I said, "Let's find out." I dialed her number and explained our problem.

"Put him on," said my *abuela*.

"Someone wants to talk to you," I told Dr. Sincere, practically shoving my phone into his face.

Curiosity got the better of him, and he answered it with a wary "Hello?"

I couldn't make out what Abuelita said, but judging by the way the scientist's face winced and flushed, it wasn't exactly a song of praise.

"Yes," he said. "Uh-huh. Well, I—no . . . no, I haven't forgotten. But the—"

His blinks started up again, faster this time, and Dr. Sincere stared down at his desktop. Benny caught my eye and mimed cracking a whip. I smothered a smile. Abuelita may have been sweet to us, but make no mistake: she was a force to be reckoned with.

"Well . . . if—if you insist." The scientist now looked

like a truant in the principal's office. I almost felt sorry for him. Almost.

"I will, Margarita," he said. "All right. You too."

"Well?" said Benny.

Handing me back my phone, Dr. Sincere said, "Your grandmother can be very persuasive."

"You don't know the half of it," I said. "Now tell the truth. What's up with those giant bugs? What do they want? Where do they come from?"

Smoothing the front of his wrinkled safari jacket, the scientist said, "They're an experiment gone very, very wrong. And it's all my fault."

Chapter Fifteen

Army-geddon

BENNY AND I shoved the junk off of a couple of office chairs and sat down to listen to Dr. Sincere's tale. By the time he was halfway through, I felt glad we were sitting.

"Back during the Cold War, our country sought every advantage against the Russians," he said. "We even worked on a Star Wars program to blast their missiles out of the sky."

Benny's mouth fell open. "Wow, you mean we've got our own Death Star?"

"Eh, not exactly," said Dr. Sincere. "At any rate, I worked on Project Hive at Vandebunt Army Base outside of town. We were trying to harness the power of insects, to use them to defend our country."

"What, like an attack force of fire ants?" I asked, skeptical.

Benny smirked. "I prefer the stinkbug bomb squad."

Waving his hand as if to erase our comments, the scientist said, "We explored all those ideas and more. But each had limitations. For one thing, the insects wouldn't obey commands; they had minds of their own."

"Sounds like my sister," I said.

Dr. Sincere sighed, combing his fingers through his thinning hair. "The wasps were so bad-tempered, they attacked their handlers. The cockroaches ate everything but wouldn't fight. And all the assassin bugs wanted to do was kill each other."

Benny fidgeted. "So, the program didn't work?"

"At first," said the scientist, his gaze sliding away from ours.

"And then?" I prodded.

"Then," he said, "I hit on the idea of combining human DNA with that of insects."

I nudged Benny. "Sounds like a comic book."

Pulling at his collar, Dr. Sincere said, "Yes, well, the DNA wasn't terribly compatible. Most of the human-insect combinations died quickly—our scorpion man lasted the longest, poor fella."

Benny nudged me back. "Scorpion Man? Now that *definitely* sounds like a comic book."

That reminded me. I glanced around the floor for more of those little creepy-crawlies. Luckily, none showed.

"But you're talking about the failures," I said. "What happened with the mantises?"

"And shouldn't that be 'mantii'?" said Benny. "Or 'manteese'?"

With a seasick smile, the bug expert rose from his chair and paced away from us. "You don't understand. There was so much pressure to succeed, we took some dreadful risks." Dr. Sincere turned to face us, bringing his palms together at his lips, almost as if he was praying.

"And something went wrong," I guessed.

He sagged. "I was reckless. I thought if we dosed some of the hybrids with radiation, they might mutate."

I met Benny's gaze. "Mutants," we breathed.

Dr. Sincere's lips pressed together. "We were desperate for results, so I blasted the mantid hybrids with massive amounts of radiation. We hoped it would accelerate changes. But we had no idea what would happen."

"Well, duh," said Benny. "Anyone who's read a comic book knows that. Radioactive mutants are unpredictable."

I nodded solemnly. "That's a fact."

Jamming his hands into his pockets, the scientist stared out the window as if watching a movie of his past. "They grew at an astounding rate," he said. "First to the size of a house cat, then of a goat. By the time the base was shut down, the mantids were as tall as you."

"But these things at our school are much more than just big bugs," I said, shifting in my seat to watch him. "They're actually imitating our lunch ladies."

Mr. Sincere grimaced, and the blinking resumed. "Some,

er, chameleon DNA was added to the mix. Soon we found these . . . mutant mantises could take on the appearance of any creature they inhabited."

"Inhabited?" I asked.

"Er . . . took over. Like a virus. It happened with cats, raccoons, and, um, some larger beings."

Benny's eyes found mine. I gasped. It was hard to catch a breath. Now we knew what had happened to our real cafeteria workers.

"Oh, those poor ladies," I said. "I knew they weren't themselves!"

Clutching his stomach, Benny said, "That's awful. Maybe you're right, Carlos—maybe we should tell someone, like the army. Or the marines."

"No, no!" The scientist hurried over to us, his eyes as big as tortillas. "You mustn't!"

"Give us one good reason why not," I said.

He bit a knuckle. "I, er, I can cure them. With time, I can create a serum that will freeze the mantids in their human form. They may not ever be quite the people they used to be, but at least they'll be harmless."

"Seriously?" said Benny.

"Absolutely."

"How long will it take?" I asked.

"Just a few days in the lab," said Mr. Sincere. "That's all I need."

I hesitated. "Well . . ."

"That's excellent," said the scientist. "Thank you both."

Crossing his arms, Benny said, "We haven't said yes yet."

Mr. Sincere spread his hands. "But what more do you need?"

"More answers." Benny scowled, rising to his feet. "You said that the army base was shut down years ago. What happened to the mantises—mantids, mantii, whatever?"

Examining his scuffed shoes, the scientist cleared his throat. "Abandoned," he said, "just like the base."

I jumped from my chair. "Shut the front door! You just walked away and left your creepy experiments behind?"

"It's not my fault," Dr. Sincere snapped. "I was only following orders."

"So were Darth Vader's storm troopers," said Benny. "But that doesn't make it right."

"Yeah," I said.

The bug expert hung his head again, his fire fading. "We gassed the laboratories, locked the door, and left. We thought they'd all been destroyed."

"You thought wrong," I said. "And now these things are taking over our school."

"What do they want?" asked Benny, taking a step toward the scientist. "To lay their eggs all over the cafeteria?"

"Actually," said Dr. Sincere, "they're sterile."

Benny frowned. "Like Bactine?"

"No, like they can't have any babies," said the bug expert, as if he was talking to a three-year-old. (Sometimes with Benny, this is the best approach.) "They'd have to find other ways to multiply."

"Never mind that," I said. "How do we figure out what they're up to?"

Dr. Sincere looked as miserable as a wet cat at a water park. He gave an apologetic shrug. "That's just it," he said. "They've been mutating for over twenty years. Who knows what they want?"

"*Ay-yi-yi,*" I muttered.

Nervously, the scientist picked up one of the butterfly nets and turned it in his hands. "I . . . Please, I want to develop the serum. I feel responsible."

"That's because you *are!*" Benny blurted.

The bug expert started to say something in his defense, then abruptly shut up.

"So, do it," I said, leaning forward. "Find the cure that's going to give us back our lunch ladies."

"I will," Mr. Sincere promised. "I'll get right on it."

"Meanwhile, we'll work on this from our end," said Benny.

"But we need some advice first," I said.

"Name it," said the scientist.

I raked a hand through my hair. "How do we stop these mutants? What are their weaknesses?"

Dr. Sincere picked at the butterfly net. "Well, mantids do have natural predators," he said. "Frogs, monkeys, birds."

Benny snorted. "To eat these suckers? The frog would have to be the size of an SUV."

"A condor is the only bird big enough to take them on," I said. "And they're endangered."

With a grimace, the scientist said, "Er, the mantids do have one weakness."

"What?" I said.

"Tell us," said Benny.

Dr. Sincere reached out a finger and ran it along the praying mantis photo. "They don't self-regulate well."

I cocked my head. "Um, in English?"

"They can't control themselves," said the scientist. "Especially around food. They could, potentially, eat until they explode."

Goose bumps erupted on my arms as a thought occurred. "But what do they eat?" I asked.

One of Dr. Sincere's big hands reached up and scrubbed his jaw. His eyes shifted. He looked like he was trying to keep his mouth from talking.

"What is it?" Benny demanded.

The bug expert's shoulders hunched. "Normally, mantids will eat other insects, perhaps even a lizard or mouse."

Turning to me, Benny said, "So that explains what happened to all the pests in the cafeteria."

I nodded slowly. A bad feeling was burbling up in my stomach, like the aftereffects of too many refried beans. "But these are *mutant* mantises," I said, pinning the scientist's gaze with my own. "What do *they* eat?"

He squirmed. "Theoretically?"

"No," I said, "really, truly."

Dr. Sincere turned his palms up. "Anything smaller than them."

My stomach gave a twist, then tied itself into a sheepshank knot. I had trouble swallowing. "A—and what's smaller than them?" I choked out.

"Us?" said Benny in a voice as tiny as Jiminy Cricket's lunchbox.

"Us," I said.

As the light dawned, Benny's horrified gaze found mine. "So the only way to stop them . . ." he began.

". . . is to feed them the entire student body of Monterrosa Elementary," I finished.

"Heh," said Benny. "I'm sure Principal Johnson won't mind."

Dr. Sincere cleared his throat. "Well, not the *entire* student body."

"What do you mean?" I asked.

"When it came to mealtimes, our mantids showed a distinct preference for males."

"Males?" I gulped, turning to my best friend.

"So you know what that makes you and me, Carlos?" he said.

I nodded, and grabbed my gut.

"Bug bait," I said.

Chapter Sixteen

Crimes and
Sister Meaners

WERE WE WORRIED? Hey, you're talking about
two guys who have laughed at danger, who have
taken the worst the supernatural world could
dish out and come up swinging.

We were terrified.

Seriously, I defy you to stay cool when you discover
you're the main course on some mutant's lunch menu. And
to top it off, our task seemed impossible. Using only our
wits, we had to defeat three superstrong, supertricky predators who wanted nothing more than to snack on our giblets.
It would've been easier to arm wrestle a T. rex.

After leaving Dr. Memphis Sincere, Benny and I pedaled homeward, shaking like guava jelly on the San Andreas
fault. Yes, the scientist was working on a way to cure the

lunch ladies, but until he succeeded, it was up to us to stop the giant bugs. We needed a plan, and we needed it quick.

Who knew when the mutated cafeteria workers would switch from feeding us to feeding *on* us? And if the vanished boys were any indication, they might have already started.

My stomach went all queasy at the thought.

"What do we do?" Benny asked. Our shadows fled before us as we rolled down the streets in the late-afternoon sunshine.

"I don't know, but we'd better do it quick," I said. "Those mutant freaks have been feeding us boys all that good stuff to fatten us up."

"And what about the girls?" said Benny.

I considered. "Well, they're getting different food, right?"

"Right."

"Maybe even something with bugs in it, so . . ."

"Ooh." Benny's eyes widened. "Do you think the lunch ladies are trying to turn the girls into mutants like them?"

"Maybe . . ."

"I mean, I've always thought girls were freaks," he said, "but this is ridiculous."

Leaning into the corner as we rounded Jasper Street, I said, "It makes sense. Dr. Sincere did say the mutants were sterile. How else could they make more of themselves?"

Benny shivered. "Gross. It does explain why the girls are getting so aggro, though."

I nodded, seeing it. "Bit by bit, the mantises are turning

them into heartless predators. No wonder Tina acted like such a jerk."

"We've got to stop them."

"No duh," I said. "Let's go figure out how."

When we reached my house, Veronica and her little friends Maya and Hannah were making a ruckus—great, *more* aggressive girls—so Benny and I retreated to the tree fort for some serious thinking.

Our tree-fort clubhouse is basically a platform in one of the oak trees that stands in a field between Benny's house and mine. Ever since we were old enough to climb, it's been our retreat from the world. But this time, our retreat was short-lived.

I slumped against the tree trunk. "*Ay huey*, are we in trouble."

"Trouble is practically our home address," Benny agreed, picking at the splintered edge of one of the boards. "The question is, what are we gonna do about this?"

I tapped my chin, thinking. "Well . . . flies get stuck in flytraps, so maybe we can make some kind of giant, sticky mantis trap?"

Benny shook his head. "With what—tar? Quick-drying cement? They're so big—it'd never hold them."

"Okay, genius," I said, "then what's your idea?"

He cocked his head. "Um . . . what if we . . . flooded the kitchen with water and drowned them?"

"Perfect," I said, "except (a) it'd take forever to fill that room with a hose; and (b) if those missing kids are still alive and locked in the pantry, we'd drown them too."

"Oh, yeah," said Benny.

I straightened as an idea hit me. "Hey, what about that old bear trap of your dad's?"

Benny made a game-show buzzer sound. "Wrong-o. They're not as dumb as were-hyenas, and there's three of them."

I tugged on my hair. This being a hero and coming up with plans was harder than it looked.

"I know," said Benny. "We could light them on fire!"

"And burn down the cafeteria? Maybe the whole school?"

"Bad idea?"

"Bad idea."

After a long pause, Benny looked up. "So where does that leave us?"

I sighed. "In deep, deep doo-doo. Dr. Sincere better come up with that cure soon."

"There's got to be some way we could—"

At that moment, a shout from below penetrated our gloom.

"Hey, doody-heads!" It was my sister, Veronica. And, judging by the giggles, both of her friends.

"Go away!" I yelled. "We're busy."

"It's our turn for the tree fort," said Veronica.

I poked my head over the platform's edge and gave her my death-ray stare. "We were here first. And besides,

Mom says you can't climb up here until you're seven."

Apparently my death-ray stare was losing strength. My sister put her hands on her hips and mustered up her own glare. "That's only three weeks away. And b'sides, I'm a great tree climber."

"Beat it, little blister," I said. "Boys only."

She crossed her arms and stuck out her lower lip, a pose I recognized from her TV show. Her friends copied her. "Girls can do anything boys can," said Veronica.

"More!" said her friend Maya.

"Not in this tree fort," Benny said.

This wasn't a new struggle. Veronica had been trying to get up here for over a year. Usually, she just made herself obnoxious for a while (an easy thing for her) and then went away.

Not this time.

"Come on, girls," she said. "Let's take this tree back from these doody-head boys!"

"*Yarrgh!*" her friends cried.

All three of them charged us like a pint-sized army. With growls and grunts, they began to actually scale the trunk.

"Hey!" I shouted. "Get down from there."

"No!" Veronica's teeth were gritted, and the light in her eyes was as crazy as a hatful of doodlebugs. She climbed a couple feet up, then slid partway back.

"Get down now, or I'm telling Mom," I said.

Benny motioned at the broomstick we kept up there for knocking down acorns and stuff. "You want the stick?"

I watched Hannah slip back down. "I don't think we'll need it," I said.

"When I get up there, I'm throwing you guys over!" screeched my sister, regaining some ground.

"And then we'll bite off their heads and suck out their guts," said Maya, her blond hair dancing.

"Yeah!" growled Hannah.

I met Benny's eyes. "Okay, is it just me, or is this getting weird?"

"It's getting weird," he said.

I picked up the broomstick and was considering using it, when a welcome call cut into the grunting and growling below. "Kids! Dinner!" my mom yelled from the backyard.

"Hear that?" I said. "Time for all munchkins to go inside."

"Grrr," said Veronica. The whites of her eyes were showing.

"Your sister is creeping me out," said Benny.

"You're not alone," I said.

The little girls below us snarled some more and gained another foot or so. I don't know where it would have ended if my mom hadn't appeared at the back gate.

"Didn't you hear me?" she said. "Come inside, it's dinnertime."

Quick as a flash, Veronica and her friends slid down the trunk. They turned to beam angelic smiles at my mom.

"Were you just climbing that tree?" Mom asked.

"Us? No," said my little sister. "We're pretending."

"Playing monsters," Maya added helpfully.

I looked from Benny to the little girls. They were doing something more than just playing. And if we didn't put a stop to it in a hurry, I might find myself the big brother to a mini mutant mantis.

Loads of fun for the whole family, I thought.

Until she ate me, that is.

Chapter Seventeen

My Sister the Mini-Mantis

DINNER THAT NIGHT was . . . interesting. Not the food, which was yummy—fish tacos, rice, and salad—but the conversation. Mom started it off.

"So, Carlos, I hear you had to stay after school today," she said, taking a sip of water.

Inwardly, I cursed. I'd forgotten that principals sometimes like to talk with parents, especially when their kid is in trouble.

"Ha ha, detention!" Veronica singsonged.

"Um, yeah," I said. "But it's really no big deal."

"Detention?" My father looked up from his rice. "Why did they give you detention?"

"Carlos started a food fight!" squealed Veronica.

"A food fight?" my mom echoed. "And this is the first we're hearing of it?"

I glared at my little sister. "That's a bit of an exaggeration."

Veronica's wide smile was full of malice. "The whole school got into it. Lunch was *allll* over the place. What a mess!"

"Carlos?" said my dad.

"We, uh . . . okay, it did get a little out of hand." I took a bite of salad.

A vertical crease appeared between Mom's eyebrows. "We didn't raise you to be the kind of boy who starts food fights. You know better than that." Her eyes narrowed. "Was it Benny?"

My chest felt tight. Although my mom was always polite to my best friend, she blamed him for most of the trouble I got into. Accurate though that might be, I didn't like it.

"It was both of us," I said firmly. "We were protesting some changes at the cafeteria."

Dad spread his hands. "Surely there's a better way to protest," he said. "Ever hear of petitions?"

"He threw Jell-O!" my sister cackled. "Doody-head!"

"Language," Mom warned her.

My jaw tightened. I couldn't very well tell my parents that petitions wouldn't stop the mutant lunch ladies from taking over our school and eating all the boys. But maybe it was time I filled them in on some of the weirdness. I decided to start small and see how things went.

"We had to take a stand," I said. "The lunch ladies are feeding the boys something different from the girls."

My mom cocked her head. "Different how?"

"The girls are getting protein and healthy stuff, while we're eating junk food," I said, oversimplifying a bit. Well, quite a bit.

Mom's frown deepened. "That's not right. Growing boys need protein too, and nobody should be filling up on junk food."

I leaned forward. "But that's not all. It's affecting the girls' behavior."

"What do you mean?" my dad asked around a mouthful of fish taco.

"They're getting rude and aggressive," I said. "Haven't you noticed how Veronica's been acting?"

My sister made a wounded, innocent expression that looked rehearsed. She put a hand to her chest. "Me?"

Mom patted her arm and chuckled. "Don't be silly. She's just our little diva."

Veronica gave Mom a wide, fluttery-eyed smile. But the lightning-fast glare that hit me when Mom looked away revealed her true nature.

Dang, my sister was a better actress than I'd thought.

"But she—" I spluttered.

"Now, Carlos," said my mom, "cut your sister some slack. She's going through a lot of changes."

You have no idea, I thought.

"Okay, she's adjusting to being an actress," I said. "I get it, but this is different. She's been acting deranged."

Dad shot me a look over his glasses. "Envy doesn't become you, Carlos. I'm sure you're exaggerating," he said.

"I'm not—" I sputtered. "This is about *her*, not me. She doesn't even care that her friend Justin is still missing."

With a smile that made my scalp prickle, Veronica said, "Oh, he'll turn up soon."

In a casserole, I thought.

"Carlos, your sister's experiencing an exciting, challenging time," said my dad. "We expect you to look out for her, not resent her."

"I'm trying!" I cried. "But you just won't listen!"

Mom raised her eyebrows. "Now who's being dramatic?"

I groaned and let my head sag over the back of the chair. This was like trying to teach a warthog to dance, but even less productive. "Look, forget Veronica for a second. The girls at my school have been getting rough—talking trash, beating up boys."

"In other words, behaving like boys do?" said my mom.

"Yeah, but it's—"

"Mijo." Her understanding smile only set my teeth on edge. "They're just asserting themselves and breaking out of stereotypical gender roles."

I shook my head. "But you—"

"Girls are a lot more empowered these days," my dad said, taking another bite of taco.

"Plus, those hormonal changes hit them earlier and earlier," Mom said. "I'm sure that's all it is."

I didn't even want to know what "hormonal changes" were. But I knew when I was wasting my time. If my parents didn't even believe the simple stuff, they would never be able to handle mutant cannibal lunch ladies. I threw up my hands. "Fine, whatever. Can I be excused? I've lost my appetite." And any hope for the future, I thought.

My dad waved me away. "Sure thing, *chamaco*. Just don't watch TV. We'll talk later about that detention."

I pushed back from the table, carrying my plate. As I stood to go, Veronica checked that Mom and Dad weren't watching. Then she flashed a devilish smile and clacked her little teeth together, *chomp-chomp-chomp*.

The fine hairs on my arms stood up. This whole mantis thing was getting *way* too personal.

Despite spreading crumpled paper all over my floor (to warn of any midnight visits by my mutating sister), I didn't get much sleep that night. Small wonder. Now that Benny and I knew what we faced, we had to step up our efforts. More than anything, I wanted these mantis monsters out of my school and out of my life, pronto.

Benny had an idea. (It happens sometimes.) He was hoping, if we got to school early enough, we might catch the mutant lunch ladies sleeping, and dispose of them quickly. We'd tie them up and keep them from hurting any more kids. Of course, that meant *we* had to be awake when we were usually sleeping.

Way too early the next morning, something went *tap-tap-tap* on my window. I responded with a foggy "Whassamatta?" and sat up. Sometime during the night, a piece of paper had gotten stuck to my face, probably with my drool.

Peeling it off, I went to open the window for Benny. And of course, I stepped all over the crumpled paper covering my floor.

"Ready to be the early bird?" said Benny. His face was scrubbed and beaming.

"Ready to go back to sleep," I said. "But come in anyway."

Benny eyed all the papers. "I like what you've done with the place."

He sat on my bed reading a comic book while I did the speed version of getting ready for school. By the time I finished making myself a sandwich for lunch, my dad shuffled into the kitchen looking like a zombie.

"Whuzza?" he said. My dad barely can speak before he gets his morning coffee. I take after him.

"Going to school early," I said, "with Benny."

He yawned and scruffled his hair. "Wazza?"

"Big project. Later, Dad." I dropped my sandwich and an apple into a brown bag and headed out.

"Whavvyu," he grunted, kissing the top of my head as I passed.

"Me you too," I said.

Retrieving our bikes, Benny and I set off for school. The air was as chilly as a headwaiter at a fancy restaurant, and the birds chirped like mad, enjoying an all-you-can-eat bug buffet. I wished they'd come eat *our* giant insects.

My jaw dropped. An *idea*!

"Wait, birdseed!" I said, slamming on the brakes.

"Um . . . cucumber?" said Benny.

I turned to look at him. "What?"

"I thought we were doing word association. That's the first thing that came to mind."

I blinked. "No, we *need* birdseed. Where can we get some this time of the morning?"

"Try my garage," said Benny.

Chapter Eighteen

Zero Dark Birdy

WHEN WE REACHED school, only two cars sat in the lot. The front office was as dark as an undertaker's belly-button lint. But we heard the wheels of Mr. Boo's janitorial cart squeaking down the corridors, somewhere out of sight.

I led the way to the cafeteria and tried the outer door. Locked. We circled around to the kitchen and noticed a light shining through the window.

"Bummer, they're awake," said Benny.

"Good, they're home," I said, reaching for the first bag of birdseed. Ripping open the top, I began to scatter handfuls of the seed on the ground in front of the closed door.

Within seconds, a few sparrows discovered the feast. Word spread quickly. A minute or so later, the ground was thick with birds. Their chirps were nearly deafening.

"Very generous," said Benny. "So what's the plan?"

I emptied the last of my bag, tossing seeds right up against the door's threshold. "Remember how we decided only a condor was big enough to prey on giant mantises?"

"Yeah."

"What if instead of one big bird, we had lots of little birds?" I said. "That should keep the lunch ladies busy for a while."

Benny grinned. "Yeah!" He fished the second bag out of his backpack and began scattering the seeds.

"Wait," I said, "I've got a better idea. Give me a fistful and get ready to heave the rest inside when the door opens."

"Check you out," Benny said, "Mr. I've-Got-a-Plan."

He prepared for action while I tried the doorknob. Finding it locked, I rapped on the door as hard as I could.

More birds swirled down from the skies. By this point, the ground was practically a feathered carpet, with finches, robins, doves, crows, and jays crowding right up to our feet. A couple of hungry sparrows even fluttered around my seed-filled fist.

I pounded on the door again. This time a stiff voice called, "What? I am coming."

When the door opened wide, Benny and I cast handfuls of birdseed right into the round face of Mrs. McCoy. She spluttered and retreated a few steps, raising her arms defensively. I caught just a flicker of her mantis form as she transformed in surprise, then switched back.

That was all it took.

Suddenly the sky grew thick with wings, as the birds sensed their favorite food and decided to help themselves. They zoomed at the lunch lady in a mismatched flock. I don't know if they smelled her, or glimpsed her transformation, or what.

But any way you cut it, the birds were hungry for bug.

"Go get 'em!" Benny cried.

The mutant lunch lady screamed as the first wave of feathered foes plowed into her like a pack of parents at a pre-Christmas sale. Pecking wildly, their little beaks began to draw blood. Mrs. McCoy batted at them. She staggered back, back . . .

And just like that, she changed into a jumbo-size praying mantis.

Benny and I gasped and cowered. No way could we have tied up something that big and strong. But the birds weren't bothered. If anything, they redoubled their attack.

That's when Mrs. McCoy went on the offensive.

Her sharp forelegs darted out, spearing bird after bird. Her triangular head snapped, gulping down attackers left and right like a hungry tourist with a pupu platter.

"Hang in there, birdies!" I called.

But the tide had turned.

Some of the smaller birds scattered. The monster that had mimicked Mrs. McCoy made three loud clicks and a high keening sound. In a handful of heartbeats, two more

giant mantises appeared behind her, mandibles clacking. One joined her in chowing down on our feathered friends.

The other rushed the door.

"Gah!" I cried, backpedaling. This was *our* attack—the lunch ladies weren't supposed to come after *us*.

Benny hurled his half-full seed bag into the huge bug's face and danced away from the door. The mantis didn't even blink. It stared at us with its enormous, soulless eyes, and glanced past us at something. Then it hissed once and slammed the door.

Thoroughly spooked, Benny and I bolted. We put a playground's worth of distance between us and the mutant freaks before we slowed down.

"Wow," I said, catching my breath, "that didn't go quite the way I'd pictured it."

"Y-you think?" said Benny.

I wagged my head. "Dang, those things are hard to kill."

Just then, I noticed our school custodian and his cart near the corner of the nearest building.

"Hey, dudes!" called Mr. Boo. He motioned to us to join him, so we did. Then he made a big gesture at the sunrise. "As the Beatles say, Here comes the sun, and I say, it's so tight."

"Um, right," I said. My legs were still trembling.

The custodian wore jeans and a striped blue-and-green hoodie like surfers bring back from Baja vacations. His tied-back mane of gray-blond hair was still damp.

"S-s-surf s-s-session this morning?" Benny stuttered. His eyes were wider than the blue Pacific.

"Wow, you guys should be detectives or something," said Mr. Boo.

I winced. "Or something. Only we're not so hot at it." I cut a glance at the cafeteria to make sure nothing bug-related was coming our way. All clear.

The lanky custodian speared two candy wrappers from the ground without even looking. "Don't sell yourself short. You were right about the pantry."

Benny and I perked up a little. "You checked it out?" he said.

"Did you find the missing kids?" I asked, shifting from foot to foot.

Mr. Boo shook his head. "No, but I found out that the lunch ladies changed the locks—without telling me."

"Really?" I said.

Tucking a stray lock of hair behind his ear, the custodian said, "And when I told them that all lock changes should go through the Boo, they apologized. But not like they meant it."

"Did they give you a duplicate key?"

Mr. Boo frowned. "No. Every time I asked, they kept changing the subject. You know, I never did get it."

Benny gave a little cough. "Something's going on in there."

We exchanged meaningful looks. They said something

like *Should we tell him? No, what if the lunch ladies go after him too? Let's let Dr. Sincere do his thing and keep Mr. Boo out of danger.*

Amazing how much a look can convey if you've known someone a long time.

"Any chance you can open that door somehow?" I asked. "Maybe when they're not around?"

Shrugging a shoulder, Mr. Boo said, "Not without a locksmith, and that has to be approved by Mrs. Johnson."

"Who thinks the lunch ladies can do no wrong," I said.

Stumped, I rubbed my chin and gazed out across the schoolyard. By now, my heart rate was returning to something like normal. A couple of teachers had opened up their rooms, and a cluster of early-bird students headed for the swings. School was coming to life for the day.

We'd run out of time to fight the monsters without getting innocent kids caught in the cross fire.

"Could you sneak a locksmith in," said Benny, "just this once?"

"Normally, I might try," said Mr. Boo, "but not today."

I cocked my head. "Why not today?"

The custodian pointed at a poster on the wall. "After-School Bake Fest," he said. "Don't you listen to the daily announcements?"

Benny gave me a blank look. "Must have missed that," he said.

"Maybe we had one or two other things on our mind," I said.

Heads close together, we scanned the poster. It announced that the PTA was holding a massive bake fest this afternoon in the cafeteria to raise money for the lunch program. AND OUR OWN LUNCH LADIES WILL BE PROVIDING THE TASTY TREATS! it proclaimed.

A bad feeling stomped its way across the pit of my stomach like a rhino in golf cleats. The bake fest! Of course. That was when the mutants would make their big move and start chowing down on students. I just knew it.

"That must be Mrs. Ponytail's project," I mused.

"Who?" said Benny and Mr. Boo.

"You know," I said, "the nasty PTA mom with the ponytail? The one who's always hanging around the cafeteria?"

Light dawned in the custodian's eyes. "Ah, you mean Mrs. Kato. She *is* a little scary . . . but cute."

"Ewww," said Benny and I simultaneously.

"Do you know if she's dating again after her divorce?" he said.

"Ewww!"

I cut in. "That's not the point here. The point is that the lunch ladies are up to something evil—"

"Well, we don't know they're *evil*," said the custodian.

"Oh, yes, we do," said Benny and I together.

Mr. Boo blinked.

"And they'll probably open up a can of, um, whatever trouble they've been brewing at today's bake fest," I said. I didn't want to reveal too much, but I did want Mr. Boo to be on his guard.

The custodian frowned. "We don't know that."

"Yes, we do," said Benny and I together.

I raked a hand through my hair. "So that gives us just a few hours to come up with something better than spreading a bunch of birdseed to distract them."

"Don't beat yourself up, Carlos," said Benny. "It could've worked."

"Birdseed?" said Mr. Boo.

I shook my head. "Never mind."

He leaned on his trash spear and eyed us. "Dudes, I get the feeling that there's a lot more going on than you're telling me."

"There is," Benny said, "but you really don't want to know."

I leaned forward. "Still, there is one thing you could do. . . ."

"Oh yeah?" said Mr. Boo.

"Find some way to unlock that pantry," I said. "We've got to know what's inside. Could be those missing kids."

"Or the makings of some evil plot," said Benny.

"Or a boatload of canned beans," said Mr. Boo.

"Whatever it is," I said, "we need to know. People's lives may depend on it."

"You can count on me," said the janitor.

"Like a six-foot abacus," said Benny. We both gave him a strange look. "Come on," he said. "That was funny. Abacus, counting?"

"Say good-bye, Benny," I said.

"Good-bye, Benny," he said.

Even mellow Mr. Boo sighed.

Chapter Nineteen

Trash of the Titans

SOMEHOW, the morning passed, as full of tension as a steel-spring factory. Every spare moment between lessons, Benny and I traded notes on stopping the lunch ladies. Our solutions got wilder and wilder.

Smash them with a giant flyswatter was one of Benny's more out-there ideas.

Put superglue on an anvil, get them stuck to it, and drop it down a mine shaft was one of mine.

All great—if this were a cartoon.

The clock was ticking.

And we still hadn't heard a word from Dr. Sincere. I was seriously wondering whether Benny and I would have to handle this giant bug problem all by ourselves.

Meanwhile, our class was getting weirder and weirder. When Mr. Chu put on an actual knight's helmet to tell us about the Middle Ages, quiet Zizi Lee rolled her eyes and boomed, "The Middle Ages are *bo*-ring. Makes me want to go knighty-knight."

Tyler Spork's eyes goggled. "She's stealing my lines," he huffed to Big Pete. "Not fair!"

When Mr. Chu read to us from *James and the Giant Peach*, using fun character voices, Cheyenne and Amrita mocked him and threw spit wads. By lunchtime, nearly half the girls in class had visited the time-out corner—and for things that us boys were normally busted for.

Just before lunch, Tina Green stood up and announced, "Girls, let's ask Mrs. Johnson for a woman teacher. Men just don't cut it."

The girls cheered and hooted.

Mr. Chu's jaw nearly hit the floor. But the lunch bell rang before he could send Tina to the time-out corner, so he just massaged his temples and waved everyone out the door. I felt sorry for him. The best teacher in school, and half his class was sassing him.

"Don't feel bad," I told him on the way out. "It isn't you; it's the girls."

"You're still awesome," Benny said.

Our teacher eyed Gabi and Emma shoving boys out of their way at the door. He shook his head. "Maybe it's hormones."

We left before he could tell us what hormones were. Some mysteries are best left unexplored.

Since we didn't dare go through the cafeteria line, Benny and I ate our brown-bag lunches in a quiet corner of the playground. All around us, the world had turned upside down. Girls were hogging the basketball courts, cutting in line for tetherball, crowding guys off the baseball diamond, and just generally acting up.

"Look at that," said Benny. "It's disgusting."

I shrugged a shoulder. "It's what us boys always do, only more so."

"Yeah, but . . ." He trailed off. "Okay, I get your point. It's not right when we do it either. But still—"

"I don't care about right or wrong," I said. "I just want our old school back."

Benny gulped down the last of his fried tofu sandwich, belched, and balled up his lunch bag. "Any brilliant ideas? 'Cause I'm drawing a blank."

I bit my lip. I was almost desperate enough to try Benny's stupid-dangerous plan of burning down the cafeteria to flush the mantis ladies out. "Too bad the birds didn't work. They really had that Mrs. McCoy monster going."

Benny chucked his trash in the bin and gave a rueful grin. "Yeah, until she and the other one started chowing down on them. Man, they ate like they'd never stop."

"Never stop . . ." I mused.

"I bet if you put one of those mutant mantises in an eating contest, they'd win for sure, hands down."

"Eating . . ."

"They'd even beat Joey Chestnut. Heck, they'd probably *eat* Joey Chestnut."

And then I saw it—a way to use the mutant mantises' strengths against them. A way to defeat them once and for all.

If we could only solve one small problem.

"Hey, Benny?"

"Yeah?"

"Where can we get our hands on a truckload of cockroaches?"

It was the sort of mission we couldn't handle on our own, no matter how resourceful and heroic Benny and I tried to be. No, for this one, we needed help. Preferably the kind that could drive a car.

Mr. Boo turned us down. Can't say I blame him. After all, we couldn't tell him the whole story, so we must have sounded a bit whacked. And we couldn't get help from our parents either. No matter how much they love you, no mom or dad will lend a hand on a project like this. Heck, it'd be hard enough getting them to even *believe* what was going on.

"Got any dirt on your big brother?" I asked Benny.

"Not enough to blackmail him into it," he said. "What about your grandma?"

"Nah." I shook my head. "For a musician, she's pretty old-fashioned. She wouldn't understand."

That left us one last choice. But unfortunately, her help came with conditions.

"No way," said Mrs. Tamasese when we called her. "I'll help, but I won't be part of you ditching school, no matter what."

"But there might not *be* a school unless we act now," said Benny.

"Tough," she said. "Education is too important. I'll pick you up right after classes end, no sooner."

"Awww," I said.

"You want my help or not?"

"Yes, please," Benny and I chorused.

In the end, we had no choice. We were out of ideas and out of options. And if we wanted to save the boys (and okay, certain girls like my sister and Tina), we had to follow Mrs. T's rules and hope we wouldn't be too late.

Somehow Benny and I made it through the next couple hours of class, though my nerves were as raw as a rug burn and Benny's eyes were practically bugging from his head. We suffered through more disruptions from the girls (but probably not as much as Mr. Chu did).

A mere ice age or two later, the bell rang. Benny and I blasted out the door before Mr. Chu could finish his usual "That's all for today, kiddos" announcement. In fact, we motored so fast I barely caught Tina's "Nerd alert!" shout.

146

But it did sting a little. Shoving our way through the hall, we made more than our share of enemies. I slammed into a wandering third grader, knocking her flat. And when a fifth-grade boy knelt suddenly to tie his shoe, Benny and I both vaulted right over him.

No matter what, we kept on moving—pushing, weaving, bobbing, and darting. At last we reached the street. As promised, a purple-and-gold van waited at the curb. On its side the words SAMOAN STRONG arched above an illustrated ocean wave that would've made Mr. Boo drool.

The side door slid open. "Hop in," said Mrs. Tamasese.

We dove into the backseat. "Drive! Drive!" Benny shouted.

The former wrestler turned from her handicapped-accessible controls. "Seat belts," she said.

Benny made an exasperated sound as we fumbled with the straps. "Can we get going, please?" I said.

"Like the wind," said Mrs. T. "Soon as you're strapped in."

"Some getaway driver you'd make," Benny mumbled.

Cupping a hand behind her ear, she said, "What's that? You say you'd rather walk?"

"Nooo!" Benny and I cried together.

At last we were buckled in. And once we were, I saw why she'd insisted. The custom van tore away from the curb, slamming us back into our seats with a squeal of tires and the stench of burning rubber. We cut off a minivan, and the mom at the wheel shook her fist.

"Amateur," muttered Mrs. Tamasese. She gunned it,

blasting us out of the neighborhood and across town in record time. "You might want to check your supplies," she said, gesturing behind us. "I think I got everything."

Benny and I pawed through the grocery sack on the floor. "Garbage bags, check," he said.

"Extra-sweet peanut butter and powdered sugar, check," I said.

"Duct tape, check."

I looked up at Mrs. Tamasese. "Thanks, we're good," I said.

With a wild swerve and a squeal of tires, she roared down the gravel road into the city dump. "And here we are," she said, slamming on the brakes. The van stood beside the Himalaya Mountains of trash.

Benny yanked open the door. "Go, go go!"

We grabbed our supplies and leaped out, staring up at the massive mounds of garbage around us. The van's automatic door slid closed.

"Get 'em, boys!" said Mrs. Tamasese. "I'll turn this baby around so we're ready to jet."

"Thanks, Mrs. T!" I waved, thinking, If only all grown-ups were so understanding.

Benny put his fists on his hips. "Now, where does a dude find Cockroach Central?"

Chapter Twenty

Van on the Run

I SCANNED THE MOUNDS of moldy clothes, old newspapers, broken appliances, scrap wood, and general household crud. Lots of junk. Very few bugs.

"Um, follow your nose," I said. "Roaches like rotting food."

Trotting along the edge of the trash mounds, we sniffed and scanned, sniffed and scanned. The minutes ticked away. By now the lunch ladies would be assembling their trays of treats. Kids and parents would be gathering in the cafeteria, where who knew what kind of mayhem was about to break loose.

If we didn't find some cockroaches quickly . . .

"Whew!" said Benny, fanning the air. "Welcome to Stinkville."

I gagged. This part of the dump was unspeakably foul. Spoiled milk, rotten meat, mushy brown bananas, and too many decomposing foods to count sent up their mingled odors. If smelling bad were a sport, this would be the World Series of Stenchiness.

In the shade of a busted fridge to our right, I spotted movement—the telltale scuttling of little brown bodies. "There!" I cried, pointing.

Benny set down the grocery bag, and I lifted out the powdered sugar, ripping open the box. I shook out trails of the sweet stuff, leading from the trash heap off to one side. Meanwhile, Benny pulled ten big black garbage bags off their roll. Working together, we smeared peanut butter

and shook more powder into the sacks, then laid them on the ground at the end of the sugar trails.

Preparations complete, we stood back and watched. A few roaches began tucking into our powdered-sugar banquet. But not enough. Not nearly enough.

"Here, roachie-roachie-roachies!" Benny called.

"It's too *slow*," I moaned.

"How do we get them to go in the bags?" said Benny, pacing back and forth.

"I dunno."

"But it's your plan!"

I glared at Benny. "In case you haven't noticed, I'm making this up as I go along. Feel free to help."

Benny held out a hand toward the bugs and made smoochy noises with his lips, like he was calling a cat. "Yum, yum, yum! Nice roaches!"

Circling around to one side, I stomped into the pile of trash, hoping to scare some of the bugs toward our bags. Benny must have had a similar idea, because he headed the other way, until he vanished behind the trash hill.

"Can you see?" I called. "Is this working?"

"Hang on," yelled Benny. Then I heard a sound like *whoomp*, followed by a crackling like cellophane being crumpled.

I stomped some more, getting rancid cottage cheese in my shoes. More roaches fled my approach, although they didn't all flee the way I wanted them to go. I began to see why Dr. Sincere's experiments with militarizing bugs hadn't worked out.

They didn't follow orders.

Suddenly a sharper scent cut through the rotting garbage—something like burning olive oil and cheese. Over by where Benny had disappeared, I spotted a column of black smoke.

"Benny!'

"Yeah?"

"Is everything all right?" I called.

"Yeah," he shouted. "But you might want to run."

I frowned. "Run? Why?"

And then I had my answer. Orange and yellow flames crested the garbage mound Benny had vanished behind.

He'd set the trash on fire!

"¡Dios mío!" I cried, scrambling over the hills of crud and making for the road.

Benny was already waiting, not far from our line of trash bags.

"Are you nuts?" I cried. "You want to burn this whole place down, and us with it?"

He held out his palms. "Relax. Most of this stuff won't even light—I had to use some old olive oil to get things going."

I spluttered. "We're gonna be in so much trouble. Why would you do that?"

Benny shrugged. "Well, you wouldn't let me burn out the lunch ladies."

"Benny!"

"And besides," he said, "it's working." He pointed to the trash bags we'd spread on the ground.

A brown tidal wave of many-legged bodies surged away from the flames, down the trash heap, and straight for our peanut-butter-lined roach palaces. I snatched up some sticks and used them to prop open the garbage bags. Benny followed suit.

Although many of the roaches ran over our shoes, up our legs (ugh!), or across the road, many more fled into the dark, peanut-buttery safety of the trash bags. In less than a minute, every sack was bulging.

"Quick!" I cried, tossing Benny the duct tape. "Close them up."

Ripping strips of tape off the roll, he and I sealed the wiggling, writhing bags of bugs as fast as possible.

"Eeugh, ugh!" I cried.

My skin crawled (literally) as I kept flicking roaches off my arms and legs. Finally, all the bags were taped closed. I raised my eyes to the trash heap and found that Benny was right: the fire hadn't spread. By now it had almost completely died out. Only wisps of greasy black smoke remained.

Like any good getaway driver, Mrs. Tamasese had

backed her van up the road to where we were. She popped the rear hatch, but did a double take when she saw what we were carrying.

"Hey!" she called. "Make sure those bags don't come open. And spread the sheets before you bring those filthy buggers into my ride."

We obeyed, and after carefully brushing off excess roaches, hefted the bags into the back of the van. The sacks weren't that heavy, but they bulged and shifted alarmingly. Benny slammed the hatch, and we jumped back inside.

"Let's roll!" Benny yelled. "Chop chop!"

After getting one whiff of the garbage-scented air inside her van, Mrs. T scowled. "I'm changing our agreement."

"No!" I cried. "You can't back out now."

Tearing down the gravel road and out onto the streets, the former wrestler cut her eyes to watch us in the rearview mirror. "Who's backing out?" she said. "I'm just adding some work to your end, to make us square."

"What do you mean?" Benny gave a suspicious squint.

"Instead of one day, you'll each give me *three* days of helping out after school."

"Done," I said. "Just hurry!"

"Already hurrying," said Mrs. Tamasese. "But if you turn this van into a roach motel, you'll be working it off at my store till you're a hundred and ninety-three."

Chapter Twenty-One

Baking Bad

MRS. TAMASESE MADE the drive in record time. I've seen jets that didn't travel that fast. Rather than dropping us by the office, she raced down the driveway that led to the trash bins behind the cafeteria. The van screeched to a halt, whipping us back and forth, and startling some crows into flight.

"Hope we're not too late." I wrenched open the door.

Visions of Veronica as a pint-size mantis monster flashed before my eyes. My insides quivered like pudding on a roller coaster. She might be a brat sometimes, but she was still my sister.

"Hurry," said Benny.

But when we opened the back hatch, I smacked my head. "Argh!"

"What?" said Benny. "Stray cockroach?"

"No. Too many bags for us to carry in one trip. We need help."

Mrs. Tamasese glanced over her shoulder at us. "Sorry, boys. This wheelchair doesn't come with roach-carrying attachments."

Scanning the area, Benny suddenly smiled. "No sweat." He pointed. "I think we've got it."

And there, as if waiting for us, sat Mr. Boo's custodial cart.

Wrestling the gray trash cans off of it, we pushed the cart over to the van. Then Benny and I loaded up the ten sacks of cockroaches, being very careful not to tear holes in the plastic.

I was about to jump out of my skin, I was so crazy with impatience. From back here, we couldn't see anybody, but the faint murmur of voices drifted from the cafeteria.

Benny gripped my arm. "Don't worry," he said. "They haven't started yet."

"How do you know?"

"We'd hear a lot less chatter, and a lot more screaming."

"Cheerful thought," I said. "Thanks."

We trundled the loaded rig around the building, to Mrs. T's cry of "Get ready to rummmble!" As we cleared the corner, I noticed a few kids and parents ambling toward the cafeteria door, and the sound of disco music thumping. A sweet, nutty smell filled the air.

Painfully slowly, the old cart squeaked its way up to

the double doors. "He couldn't oil these wheels once in a while?" griped Benny.

As we approached the entrance, I caught a glimpse of many people inside, browsing long rows of tables.

"We're not too late," I said.

And then, a figure stepped in front of us, blockading the door.

"You can't bring that in here." It was the ponytailed PTA mom, the one Mr. Boo had called Mrs. Kato. She wore a fancy green shirt, and a scowl mean enough to make a grizzly bear turn tail.

"Um, we've got a load of emergency ingredients," said Benny. "In case they sell out and have to bake more goodies."

Mrs. Kato's glower deepened. "Then why is everything in plastic garbage bags?"

"Uh . . ." Benny glanced at me.

"Because they bought in bulk. Easier to carry this way," I said.

Looking from one of us to the other, the PTA mom said, "I don't know. . . ."

I willed her not to check out the bags, which were definitely wiggling. "It's all good, really it is. Mr. Boo—um, Decker knows all about it."

In a stroke of luck, the custodian happened to be passing through the cafeteria not far from the entrance.

"Isn't that true, Mr. Boo?" Benny called.

The custodian turned our way. "Say what, dude?"

Marching over to him, the PTA mom said, "These boys claim they're bringing in baking supplies and that you know all about it."

A broad smile crossed Mr. Boo's face at the sight of her, and he smoothed back his shaggy hair like a lion in love. "Hi, Mrs. Kato," he crooned.

"Well?" she said. "I didn't see any extra orders for supplies. Are these little scoundrels telling the truth?"

We used the distraction to edge the cart through the doors. The PTA mom's back was to us, so Benny and I made pleading faces and pantomimed *Go along with it!* to Mr. Boo.

"Uh, yeah," he said. "The boys can use the cart—it's fine by me."

"But why haven't I heard about all this?" said Mrs. Kato. "Good gravy, I am head of the cafeteria committee, after all."

As we wheeled our cartload of roaches farther into the room, I made the "stretch it out" gesture to the custodian.

He grinned down at the PTA mom. "You'd have to ask the lunch ladies about that," he said. "Your hair looks great, Amber. Have you lost some weight?"

Benny and I rolled the cart toward the kitchen, trusting the custodian's flirting to provide cover for us. "I really hope this works," I said. "If the mantis monsters don't go for the bugs, Mr. Boo will never forgive us."

"No worries," said Benny. "If they don't go for the bugs, they're going for *us*. So there won't be anything left to forgive."

I wagged my head. "How do you keep such a positive attitude?"

"Just naturally sunny, I guess," said Benny.

I spared a glance for the cafeteria. The PTA moms and dads had gone all out for the event. Red construction paper and blue crepe streamers covered the walls, balloons bobbed everywhere, and an all-butter statue of Betty Crocker stood in the corner, beaming at the crowd. (Or it might have been Hillary Clinton. I'm not sure.)

At one end, two backdrops from *The Music Man* (the sixth graders' musical) framed the stage. It gave things an old-timey look. We rolled onward, searching for the lunch ladies, and hoping against hope that Dr. Sincere would show up.

He was nowhere to be found.

Kids and parents wandered up and down long tables piled with a mind-boggling amount of treats. There were cupcakes and brownies, crullers and croissants, muffins, pies, and cakes, plus every size and shape of cookie imaginable.

Despite myself, my mouth began to water.

"Wow," said Benny. His eyes were the size of Frisbees.

"Just remember they're full of evil mantis-ness," I said.

"Right, right. But still . . ."

On the far side of the room, I spotted my sister, Veronica, and her little friends in the female mob around the GIRLS ONLY table of treats. Two of the three lunch ladies lurked nearby.

"There they are," I said.

"But where's Mrs. Perez?" asked Benny. "I mean, where's the mutant mantis pretending to be Mrs. Perez?"

I scanned the crowd. "I don't know, but we've got to get all three together."

Steering toward the knot of girls, Benny and I trundled the cockroach-laden cart along the wall. I kept swiveling my head, searching for the missing mantis. Which was probably why I didn't see the lunch monitor until she grabbed the other side of the rig. We stopped dead.

"You!" she spat. It was Tenacity, the girl who'd thrown us out of the lunchroom just yesterday.

"What is this," said Benny, "National Rudeness Week? No 'hello'? No 'how's the family'?"

Tenacity pointed at the exit. "Take that trash out of here!" she snapped.

Normally, I don't do that well with conflict. I'd rather avoid it than argue. But this time, there was too much on the line.

"Our, um, trash," I said shakily, "is exactly what this school needs. Come on, Benny." Jerking the cart backward, I tried to guide it around the stubborn lunch monitor.

She latched on with both hands. "You're not going anywhere."

"Oh yes we are," snarled Benny, yanking the rig toward us.

"Oh no you're not," growled Tenacity, pulling it back.

"Are too," said Benny.

"Are not," said Tenacity.

"He can keep this up all week long," I told her, "so you better let us go."

As we tugged the cart back in our direction, I caught Benny's eye and murmured, "Zoe." No need to say anything else. The next time the lunch monitor jerked the rig away from us, Benny and I shoved with all our might.

Down went Tenacity with a squeal.

One of the great things about a longtime friend is that you develop a kind of shorthand. With just that one word, Benny knew I was talking about the time he had a tug-of-war with his sister Zoe and won the same way.

But Tenacity didn't know that.

She tumbled into a tableful of treats, making it rain brownies left and right.

"Sweet!" said Benny, offering me a fist bump.

"Literally," I said, returning it.

Our tussle had attracted attention. Several PTA parents started in our direction, but more importantly, so did all three lunch ladies. Their eyes were as full of evil as a Voldemort family reunion.

"Ready?" I asked Benny.

"Ready," he said.

"Then here goes nothing."

And with that, we powered the loaded cart straight at the monsters.

Chapter Twenty-Two

A Cockroach Orange

TIME SLOWED TO a syrupy flow. As Benny and I plowed forward, yelling our battle cry, I had time to notice a wealth of little details. . . .

The rich smell of chocolate in the air.

The cold metal of the cart's rail in my hands.

The wide eyes of a PTA dad.

The principal's glower.

And the shimmer of the lunch ladies' bodies flickering momentarily into mantis mode as they squared off against us.

I had time to think, If the sight of us makes their disguises slip, just wait till they get a load of our cargo.

Ten feet away, I shouted, "Now!" and dug in my heels.

Sneakers squeaked on the tile floor as Benny and I wrenched the handcart to a halt.

"Loose the roaches!" he cried.

With knives and forks we tore holes in the garbage bags. Instantly, the stench of the city dump poured out. Along with it rolled a foul brown tide of cockroaches, their legs and antennae wiggling like a hutful of hula dancers.

I couldn't suppress a shiver at the sight of all those nasty little bugs. Out they surged, off the cart and onto the floor. Driven mad by the scent of all those yummy treats, they scattered in every direction.

The crowd screamed.

People scooted away from the cockroaches like a pack of preschoolers escaping at bath time. PTA moms and dads leaped onto the tables, squashing cakes and smooshing pies. I saw the music teacher, Mrs. Tanaka, faint dead away. When roaches ran up his leg, the PE teacher—gruff, burly Mr. Lewis—squealed like a teenage girl at a boy-band concert.

"Nooo!" wailed the lunch ladies.

In that instant, they faced a choice: let the roaches devour all the baked goods and derail their evil plan, or blow their disguises and chow down on the pests.

Hunger won out.

In the blink of an eye, three sweet lunch ladies transformed into three giant insects.

The mob screamed even louder, hurdling tables and shoving slowpokes aside. In a blink, I saw Principal Johnson's expression turn from disapproving to amazed to terrified. Mr. Boo had snatched up a push broom to attack the roaches, but the sight of the man-size bugs froze him in his tracks.

And through it all, the disco music kept thumping.

The mutant mantis lunch ladies ignored the music and the horrified humans around them. All their eyes were on the roaches. With mandibles clicking like a flamenco dancer's heels, they dived into the brown horde.

The cockroaches were too small for the mantises to spear with their forelegs. So the mutants got creative. Ducking down, they scooped armloads of the bugs into their gaping maws.

It was revolting. It was fascinating.

It was nature in action.

Working as a team, the three monsters surrounded the cockroaches. I don't know if you've ever seen ten garbage-bagfuls of insects, but there were a *lot* of bugs on that floor. The mantises needed every scrap of their lightning-fast reflexes just to keep up.

They gobbled, they gulped, and they gobbled some more. And still the cockroaches scattered.

Benny and I had retreated to a safe distance to watch the carnage.

"It's totally gross," said Benny.

"Totally."

"But I can't look away."

I smiled. "Me neither."

For the first time in days, I felt almost at peace. Dr. Sincere hadn't come through for us, but we'd come through for our school. Nothing left to do now but watch the monsters gorge themselves and see whether his prediction was right. With any luck, I thought, our fight was over.

Silly me.

"Hey, morons!" a voice yelled.

I turned. Stomping toward us was a very ticked-off Tenacity. Behind her ranged a pack of snarling girls, including Tina, Gabi, and my sister, Veronica. Their hands were like claws, and their eyes were pools of madness.

"You bobbleheaded boys," rasped Gabi.

"You wrecked everything," growled Tina.

"And now you'll pay!" cried my sister.

She was such a little kid to be making such a big threat. I would've laughed.

But it wasn't funny.

"Uh-oh," said Benny.

"Girl power!" shrilled Tina, clenching her fists.

"Girl power!" echoed the others.

I held out my palms. "Chill, all of you!" Pointing at the mutant mantises, I said, "Your girl-power leaders aren't even girls."

"They're *women*," snarled Tenacity without looking.

"No, they're not," I said. "See? They're giant bugs!"

None of Tenacity's group even glanced that way. They just kept on coming.

"Logic isn't working," said Benny. "Let's book!"

What else could we do? We turned and booked.

Blasting past the bingeing mutants, Benny and I raced toward the kitchen at the back. By now, most of the parents and kids had cleared out, so our path was open.

I glanced back. Tenacity and her crew of crazies were giving chase. Behind them, by the door, stood Mr. Boo. His hands were full of broom, and his face was full of confusion. He wasn't the only one.

"Boys aren't supposed to run from girls," Benny panted. "It's not natural."

"Tell *them* that," I said.

It was the oak-tree standoff all over again. Only this time, we had nowhere to climb. And Mom wasn't going to save us.

Rounding the corner, Benny and I dashed along the back wall. Luckily, the girls hadn't figured out that they could split up and head us off.

Yet.

The kitchen door hung partway open. "Almost there!" I gasped.

Just as we rushed up to it, a PTA mom with a tray of cookies stepped from the kitchen into the doorway. When she saw us, and all the looniness behind us, her smile dropped so fast it must've bruised itself.

"Yaahh!" Heaving the cookie tray at Benny and me, the woman slammed the door in our faces.

I batted aside the tray and reached for the doorknob.

Locked.

Of course.

And the deranged girls were closing in.

Chapter Twenty-Three

Benny and the Sets

"**GO, GO, GO!**" I told Benny.

"I'm going!" he cried. "This is me going!"

We whirled and dodged under the out-stretched hands of Tina and Tenacity. Then we dashed back across the center of the room. If only we could escape outside, Benny and I could grab our bikes and leave these lunatics in the dust.

I glanced over at the mutant mantises. They had devoured over half of the roaches and were still going strong. All three were noticeably swollen, like someone had pumped them full of air.

Just keep eating, I thought.

As we neared the exit, Mr. Boo waved his broom at the giant insects. "Should I . . . ?" he said.

"Stay back!" said Benny.

"But be ready to sweep up the leftovers," I called.

Benny and I were just seconds away from freedom, when someone stepped into the doorway in front of us.

"Not again!" I cried.

"You two!" Mrs. Kato barred our way, buzzing with anger like wasps trapped behind a window. "You wrecked my bake sale."

We tried to slip past her, but the PTA mom was quicker than she looked. She caught Benny and me by our shirts and held us. "You'll stay right here until the principal comes."

The principal wasn't what had me worried.

"But the monsters!" I shouted. "The crazy girls!"

"Geez!" Benny struggled in vain. "Is every female at school against us?"

I twisted, but Mrs. Kato had my shirt in an iron grip.

The lunch monitor and her posse were nearly on top of us.

We were so dead.

Or were we?

"Snakeskin!" shouted Benny. (Another inside joke.)

In a flash, we popped our heads through our neck holes and slipped backward, leaving Mrs. Kato holding our shirts. Bare-chested, we sprinted the only way open to us: toward the front of the room.

Thundering up the side steps, Benny and I dashed

across the stage. Unfortunately, our pursuers had wised up and divided; a second group was heading for the stairs on the far side to cut us off. So Benny and I ducked through the red velvet curtains.

Backstage was dim, dusty, and crowded, with painted flats dangling above us and props stacked willy-nilly. And then, salvation! Over by where a bunch of ropes were tied off to cleats, I spied a side door.

"Bingo!" cried Benny, spotting it too. We made for the exit.

The curtains swirled behind us as the girls sought the opening. A few steps ahead of me, Benny pelted up to the door and tried the knob.

"Locked!" he wailed. "Nooo!"

"Mr. Boo picks *now* to be thorough?" I said.

We turned, cornered at last. Tenacity and her girls burst through the curtains in two places. The ringleader's face was lit with an evil smile.

"Now we've got you, nincompoops," she said.

"Nincompoops?" I asked Benny.

He lifted a shoulder. "I think it's the same as doody-heads."

Spreading out into a wide line, the eight or so girls began stalking toward us like tigers closing in on a tethered goat. It may have been my imagination, but it seemed like their eyes were almost glowing.

"You don't have to do this, you know," I said.

Tina growled. "Boys have been in charge too long, mistreating girls."

"And we're really sorry about that," said Benny.

"Boys should be taught a lesson," snarled Gabi.

"Is it math?" said Benny. "'Cause I love math."

Step by step, the girls kept advancing.

I held up my hands. "Okay, we're not perfect," I said.

"Hah!" said Tina.

"But that doesn't mean we deserve to be eaten."

"Eaten?" said Tenacity, like that was the last thing on her mind. But then her eyes glazed over and a weird half smile teased her lips. "Yesss. Eating your enemy makes you stronger!"

"Eating your enemy makes you stronger," echoed the other girls.

My legs quivered and my bladder threatened to let go.

The mantises' brainwashing was taking effect.

But despite the girls' bloodthirstiness, a spark of hope flared up in me. The conversion wasn't complete. These girls weren't mutant mantises—yet. And if we could survive long enough, we just might be able to make them normal again.

Or as normal as girls get, anyway.

"Can't we all just live in peace?" said Benny.

"Tear their heads off!" screeched Veronica. "Suck out their guts!"

"Yeah!" shrilled the others, taking another step closer.

"You do, and Mom and Dad will ground you for the rest of your life!" I said.

My sister blinked and frowned, like she was working out a mildly tricky math problem. Maybe I was getting through to her.

Or maybe she was just wondering whether her little hands would actually be able to rip off my head.

Another step back, and I hit the wall. One of the cleats dug into my shoulder blade, and something touched my hair. I brushed it away.

Rope.

Instinctively, I glanced up, noticing that the lines from my cleat led to one of the wood-and-canvas flats dangling above the stage.

Dangling above the deranged girls.

I groped behind me and began unwinding the rope from its cleat. "Look, I agree with you," I told the wannabe mutants. "Girls don't have it easy, but neither do boys."

"Eat the enemy!" Tenacity cried, stalking forward.

Benny, noticing what I was up to, unwound the rope from the cleat behind him. "Carlos is right. It's hard being a kid sometimes, whether you're a boy or a girl."

Tina's lip curled. "Boys' parents don't tell them, 'Don't be such a tomboy' when they're just doing what they love."

"Well . . ." said Benny.

"Boys don't get told, 'Speak in a nice, soft voice, and don't make waves,'" said Zizi.

"That's true." I felt a twinge of sympathy for them. But not enough to stop what I was doing and let them shred me.

"Maybe you should work with us, instead of twisting off our heads," said Benny. The ropes were nearly free. From the corner of my eye, I noticed the flats above jerking and swaying. A weight dragged on my line.

"Never!" snarled Tenacity. "We will put down anyone who's against us." Her hands curled into claws. Only six feet away from us, she gathered herself to spring.

I unlooped the last curl of rope. "Couldn't have said it better myself."

Tenacity crouched, teeth bared.

Then, with a squeal of pulleys, two wide, wood-framed flats came plunging down on the savage girls with a *schoooomp-whack!* Shrieks erupted. Girl-shaped lumps stirred under the painted image of a library, and someone's foot punched through the fabric.

I hoped Veronica and the rest weren't hurt, just stunned. I also hoped that this would slow them down long enough for us to escape death by munching.

Benny whooped, slapped me a high five, and took off running toward the curtains. I joined him. Within seconds, we had slipped out onto the front of the stage.

Bad move.

A pack of sixth-grade girls ambushed us. Several of them were waiting behind the curtains, and when we stepped out, they shoved us off the front of the stage. My body stiffened, bracing for impact. But rather than the hard landing I'd expected, we fell into the arms of more lunch-lady disciples.

I'm not sure, but I may have screamed.

Kicking and twisting, Benny and I fought back. But there were just too many of them. And sixth-grade girls are scary. Rough hands gripped us and dragged us along.

"To the makers with them!" someone cried. "The makers must feed!" The rest of the pack echoed the call. They hauled us down the rows of trashed tables to where the mutant mantises stood.

"Carlos!" Benny cried.

I twisted to see him. "Yeah?"

"Remember when I said I wanted to be a hero?"

"Yeah."

"I've changed my mind."

The merciless mutant wannabes carried us past trampled tarts, crushed cookies, and battered brownies. Between our captors, I caught glimpses of the rest of the room. All the other kids and parents had vanished, leaving us alone in the mess with these sadistic schoolgirls.

I clutched at one last hope. Could our plan have worked? Had the mantises finally burst?

But then I saw the mutants, still alive. Worse, they were as huge as those Easter Island statues I'd done my history report on.

Maybe the last report I'd ever do.

"Help!" I yelped, writhing. "Someone help us!"

"Anyone?" cried Benny.

But nobody was coming.

We were on our own.

And in just a second or two, Benny and I were going to learn what the inside of a mutant mantis looked like.

Up close and personal.

Chapter Twenty-Four

Bugpocalypse Now

THE PACK OF ruthless girls set us down on our feet before the monsters. Hands gripped our arms, shoulders, and necks so tightly Benny and I could barely move. We faced our fate.

And what a fate.

Now that they'd scarfed down nearly ten bagfuls of cockroaches, the three mutant mantises had swollen to alarming proportions. In fact, they were barely recognizable as mantises, looking more like six-legged green blimps. Their triangular heads were dwarfed by their massive bodies.

But they hadn't exploded. So much for Dr. Sincere's theory. And so much for his offer of help, the big faker.

"Behold the troublemakers," said a mean redheaded girl

with a fistful of my hair in her grip and a flair for the dramatic. "Feed, O Mighty Ones!"

Though clearly terrified, Benny mouthed, *O Mighty Ones?* Even to the end, he hated corniness.

The monsters ignored the redhead, instead scuttling about after the last handfuls of cockroaches. By this time, they had to shove aside the debris to find the pests' hiding places.

"Those are *our* prisoners!" cried a voice that sounded a lot like Tenacity. "Let them go!"

Mean Red turned, which meant that my head was wrenched around, since she didn't release my hair. "Finders keepers, losers weepers," she sneered.

Tenacity's fists landed on her hips. "Who you calling losers?"

"Yeah!" cried my little sister. "*You're* the losers!"

"Shut up, short stuff!" snapped a big black-haired girl.

I wanted to defend my sister, but didn't want to call attention to myself. Still, I couldn't help saying, "You shouldn't have said that."

Sure enough, Veronica hissed and surged at the other girl. Tina held her back.

"Double doody-head!" shrieked Veronica, snapping her jaws.

How about that? I thought. They're fighting over who gets to feed us to the monsters.

"Aren't we the popular ones," said Benny.

"I'd settle for being alive and ignored, if it's all the same," I said.

As we watched, words escalated into blows. Tenacity shoved Mean Red. Red took a swing at Tenacity, tugging out some of my hair along the way.

Next thing you know, the two groups of girls closed in on each other, pushing, punching, and pulling hair. Tenacity's group was smaller, but they made up for it in ferocity. I saw Tina karate-kick a sixth grader in the gut, and my own sister bit the black-haired girl's leg like a rabid terrier.

Apparently, you can turn someone into a predator, but you can't control what they prey on. These budding slayers had turned on each other.

Forgotten, Benny and I stepped away from the free-for-all. He was about to blast for the door, but I caught his sleeve.

"Wait," I said.

"Are you totally whacked? Let's bounce before they remember who they were fighting over."

I shook my head. "Look."

The three mantises had found a cache of bugs hiding beneath a fallen tablecloth. As we watched, they shoveled the last of the roaches into their greedy maws, crunching away. But they couldn't see what we could.

The monsters' swollen bodies were pulsating, expanding and contracting like a bellows. With each throb, their bodies grew bigger and bigger, like hideously warped balloons—until, just like an overinflated balloon . . .

They popped.

But that doesn't really do it justice.

To be more accurate, the mantises exploded, they went supernova, they burst like a bargain-basement piñata. One second, they were just three fatty-fat insects, and the next . . . *pow!* Bits of greenish meat, cartilage, guts, and half-digested cockroaches sprayed the room like someone had set off a bug bomb made entirely of bugs.

I had just enough time to say, "Look ou—!" when Benny and I were hit by a tidal wave of goop. The nasty, sour-smelling stuff struck us with the power of a football tackle. Down we went, right into the nearest table.

The battling girls caught the full force of the blast. It knocked them over like bowling pins, blowing them into a tangle of arms and legs and greenish glop.

For a long, long moment, all was silent, except for a wet, dripping noise. Then a voice that sounded like my sister said, "Eeww, my hair!"

I had to laugh. But as it turned out, that wasn't such a hot idea, since I got a mouthful of mantis guts. Did it taste bad? Let me put it this way: combine spoiled cauliflower, Brussels sprouts, and *escamole* (a Mexican dish made from ant larvae—really!) with rancid Limburger cheese, and you're just starting to get in the ballpark.

"Ack-ick-uck!" I hocked, and spat, and wiped my face with an arm.

Painted with green glop, Benny took one look at me and

burst out laughing. "I can't believe you ate bug goop!"

Trust a friend to comfort you in your hour of distress.

Then his face puckered like a drawstring purse as Benny got his own taste of buggy flavor. "Eeewww! Gross! This stuff is *nasty*!"

And we weren't the only ones who found the bug guts disgusting. Rising to her knees, a goop-covered Gabi grabbed her belly and clapped a hand over her mouth. Her body hunched once, twice, and then . . .

"Blaarrrgh!" She ralphed all over Tina.

Revolted, Karate Girl sprang to her feet, gave a full-body shudder, and horked up the contents of her stomach onto Mean Red's head.

From there on, it was basically Barf City. The urge to upchuck spread among the mutant wannabes like head lice in a preschool. Before long, all the girls who'd wanted to rip our heads off were helplessly losing their lunch all over each other and the cafeteria floor.

"I love a happy ending," sighed Benny.

It felt good to laugh again, this time with mouth closed. I found some dry napkins and swabbed my face. I even risked a bite of brownie to help mask the aftertaste.

Struggling to our feet, Benny and I surveyed the scene. It looked like a deeply sick giant had blown his nose all over this end of the cafeteria, and then sprinkled in some cockroach bits. And it smelled as bad as it tasted. The slime coated everything—the walls, the tables, the treats, and the queasy girls who were beginning to sit up.

"The—the makers!" cried one of them, finally noticing the mantises' remains. "They're . . . *disgusting.*"

"And gone!" wailed another.

"What do we do?" asked Gabi. "They always knew what to do."

One glop-covered head swiveled in my direction, and two brown eyes glared at Benny and me. "You! You're responsible!" snarled Tenacity weakly.

"Hey, we didn't *make* them overeat," said Benny. "It's like that commercial—know when to say when."

But the girls weren't buying it. Their leaders were gone, and they wanted someone to blame.

Us.

The gunk-ified girls lurched to their feet with murder in their eyes. Even worse, they stood between us and the exit.

I'm not sure exactly where this would've ended, but just then, a familiar lanky figure stepped into the doorway behind them with a hose in his hands.

"Always the same story," said Mr. Boo. "The kids make the mess; the janitor cleans it up."

"Huh?" said Tenacity, turning.

"In the words of the immortal Bob Dylan, Spray, Mr. Tambourine Man!" said the custodian.

And with that, he worked the hose lever, blasting high-pressure water onto me, Benny, and all the wannabe mantis girls.

Chapter Twenty-Five

Safe and Found

I NEVER THOUGHT I'd say this, but sometimes, having responsible adults around really comes in handy. By the time the custodian had finished hosing off the slime, Mrs. Johnson arrived, backed by some teachers and a few PTA parents. The girls still wanted to beat us up, but they knew the principal would never allow it. They sulked and glowered instead.

Mrs. Johnson strode over to us, being careful not to step in any puddles with her fancy kangaroo-skin boots. She wore a cranberry-colored pantsuit and a wary expression.

"Boys," she said.

"Mrs. Johnson," we replied.

She surveyed us. "You look like you've been chewed up, spit out, and stepped on."

"Yes, ma'am," we said.

The principal stroked her chin. "I assume there's some

kind of logical explanation for what I witnessed here today?"

Logical? Benny and I exchanged a glance. "Not really," said Benny.

"But we'll try," I added.

We told her about the army experiments, about the mutant mantises imitating the lunch staff, and about what we thought they were planning at our school.

Mrs. Johnson arched an eyebrow. "Mutant mantis lunch ladies?"

"Yes, ma'am," we said.

She shook her head. "This ain't my first rodeo, but giant bugs? That's a whole 'nother thing." Glancing over at the girls, Mrs. Johnson asked, "Are they in any danger?"

As the PTA and Mr. Boo continued their cleanup, Benny and I explained that the girls had had almost a week of brainwashing and some weird food that was supposed to help turn them all mantis-y. "No telling what was in it," I said. "Bug bits? Broccoli? Some kind of mantis juice? Luckily, these girls puked it all up."

Mrs. Johnson winced. "Dang. I guess that means we've got to give the rest of them an emetic."

"Emetic?" said Benny.

"Something to make them throw up," she said.

I made a face. "Every girl in the school?"

One side of her mouth curled. "You can't get lard unless you boil the hog." In answer to our blank expressions, she said, "That means, it's disgusting, but it's gotta be done."

Benny blew out some air. "Man, I'd hate to be Mr. Boo—er, Decker after they finish."

"We won't give them emetics in the hallways," said Mrs. Johnson. "What kind of school do you think this is?"

Benny was saved from answering that straight line by the appearance of Mr. Boo himself. "Hey, I drilled through the lock on the pantry," he said, "and guess what I found?"

"Pasta and canned vegetables," said Mrs. Johnson.

The lanky custodian shook his head. "Nope. Well, a few cans, maybe. No, dude, I found these three."

He gestured, and Veronica's friend Justin tottered forward, followed by our missing classmate AJ, and another kid who must have been Nathan. All three looked shakier than a tot on a ten-speed bike, and really, really glad to be free.

With a cry of relief, Mrs. Johnson rushed over and gave them all a hug. Little Justin clung to her like a baby koala to its mother.

"I—I—I thought they were g-gonna e-eat us," he stuttered, burying his face in her belly.

"Oh, sweet pea," she said. "You poor li'l thing."

Nathan's teacher hurried up to claim him. Benny and I greeted AJ, who solemnly shook our hands and thanked us. Despite their captivity, all three boys looked healthy. They might have even put on a pound or two.

"What did they do to you?" asked Benny.

"You don't wanna know," said AJ.

"Actually, we do," I said.

Our classmate shrugged, clearly uncomfortable. "They kept feeding us sweets and junk food."

"Yum," said Benny. "Lucky you!"

AJ shot him a dirty look. "And they were always experimenting on us with different foods and pinching us."

"Pinching you?" I said.

"To see if we were fat enough yet." AJ seemed queasy. "Mrs. McCoy—er . . ."

"The thing that looked like Mrs. McCoy?" I said.

"Yeah. She said they were going to serve me up in a nice cream sauce tonight." He looked a little green.

Benny clapped his shoulder. "Cheer up. At least it wasn't garlic sauce."

"You're safe now," I added.

"So"—AJ looked around—"they're really gone?"

"As gone as last year's leftovers," I said.

He gave a shaky chuckle. "Thanks for proving I wasn't crazy. And for putting a stop to those . . . things." He looked from one of us to the other. "I guess you guys really are heroes."

A warm feeling started somewhere down in my belly and made its way up to my face. I ducked my head.

"Aw, shucks," said Benny.

"Really stinky heroes," said AJ, fanning the air. "Seriously, you both need a shower. And shirts."

I couldn't argue with that.

"Yeah, well, don't think your flattery gets you out of

paying us," said Benny. "We still expect a week's allowance and a plate of your dad's cookies."

"I think I'll make that *two* plates," said AJ.

Veronica didn't much care for her vomiting session. But it did seem to calm her down some. At least she wasn't talking about ripping off my head anymore. By the time Mom came to pick us up from school, my little sister was on the road back to being her usual self.

Still a diva, yes. But at least not a cannibal diva.

After the experience, Tina seemed sullen and a bit embarrassed. Still, it was good to have my friend back. She joined us at the curb to wait for her own ride, scuffing the concrete with the toe of her sneaker.

"You feeling okay?" I asked.

Tina squinted out at the road. "I feel bad for the real cafeteria ladies, the ones who got . . . you know, eaten."

I was about to correct her and say "inhabited," the word that Dr. Sincere had used. But he'd turned out to be a big fat liar. I stared down at my hands. "Yeah. They didn't deserve that."

"Nobody does," said Benny.

The four of us were quiet for a moment, remembering the three kind, goodhearted women.

Tina broke the silence. "You know, they weren't all wrong, the mutant mantis lunch ladies."

I eyed her. "You mean, aside from the whole 'let's eat

the boys and turn the girls into giant bugs' thing?"

"Right," said Tina. "Aside from that."

"Really?"

Her face tightened. "Things aren't fair for girls today. We have limits. We have expectations to deal with."

"Like boys don't?" said Benny, wringing water from his wet T-shirt.

Tina glowered. "Zip it, Brackman. It's not the same for girls, and you know it."

"Yeah," Veronica seconded.

Benny pulled a skeptical face, but he wisely said nothing. I guess being chased by a horde of bloodthirsty girls could teach even Benny a thing or two.

"So maybe things will be different around here," I said, "now that everyone's had a taste of how the other half lives."

"Maybe," said Tina. But she seemed doubtful.

"One thing will be different, anyway," said Benny.

"What's that?" I asked.

He grimaced. "Lunch will never be the same again."

I nodded. "Because of the memories?"

"Because of the food." Benny's face looked as mournful as a dog dragged away from roadkill. "We'll never find another set of lunch ladies that serves up so much junk food."

"Unbelievable," said Tina.

Benny grinned. "Thanks. I try."

I wagged my head. "As a wise person once said: 'Zip it, Brackman.'"

Chapter Twenty-Six

Little Blister

THAT WEEKEND, our Saturday-night meal ended up being kind of a special occasion. It was Veronica's farewell dinner. Her hiatus had ended, and the next day she and Mom would head back to LA to resume Veronica's work on the TV series.

Plus, there was the whole not-getting-eaten-or-turned-into-a-mutant thing to celebrate.

Abuelita went all out for the occasion. We had squash blossom sauté, pork *carnitas*, frijoles, polenta, and more side dishes than you can count. And this time, she even let Mom help her in the kitchen.

During our first attack on this amazing spread, everyone stayed pretty quiet. (Except my dog, Zeppo, who whined for some pork and slobbered on my lap.) My dad was scooping polenta when he shook his head and half chuckled.

"I still can't believe it," he said. "Giant bugs serving lunches at Monterrosa Elementary. Sounds like a *National Enquirer* headline. Who knew the army was conducting those weird experiments just down the coast?"

"Who knew?" said Abuelita, with a secret smile.

Right after our big showdown with the mutant mantises, the army had tried to convince people that there *were* no mutant mantises—that everyone had actually hallucinated due to a gas leak.

Yeah, right.

But not much hard evidence of our bug battle remained. The goo had been cleaned up, and Dr. Sincere had removed the jars of mantis juice that he assumed the lunch ladies had been serving to girls "for further study."

And speaking of the slimy scientist, he was currently on the run, whereabouts unknown. Someone (I suspect Abuelita) had placed an anonymous phone call to the army's Criminal Investigation Command, and he bugged out (so to speak) just before their team arrived. It was only a matter of time until they caught him.

Although I'm not a vengeful guy, I hoped they would lock up Dr. Sincere for good in the most roach-infested cell they could find.

When the news vans appeared at our school after the Bugpocalypse, they had nothing to film. The mutant mantises were gone, and no one on staff would give an interview.

Mrs. Johnson's orders. I guess she was afraid of the school getting sued or something. So the news died out pretty quickly.

"From what your principal said, you and Benny were very helpful in getting rid of those creatures," said my mom.

"Yeah," I said.

"But there's something that confuses me—"

"Why is everyone making such a big deal over Carlos?" my sister cut in, pouting.

Mom sent her a "hush up" look. "If you and Benny were such a help, Carlos, then why is Mrs. Johnson giving you a week's worth of detention? She should be giving you a medal."

Forking some pork into my mouth, I said, "It's complicated."

Sometimes even heroes can't get away with releasing bagfuls of cockroaches in the school cafeteria.

My mom patted my hand. "Well, I imagine it'll be good to get back to normal." She glanced over at Veronica. "Good for both of you. Tell me, *mijo*, are you going to miss having your sister around?"

I considered Veronica, across the table. She wore not the crazed expression of a monster-in-training, but the bratty look of a little girl who wants to be fussed over. Despite all we had been through the past few days, despite her nearly munching me, she was still my sister.

"A little," I said. "It wasn't totally awful having her back."

Veronica squirmed in her seat. "And it wasn't totally awful being home with my big brother."

We exchanged a nod and went back to eating our meal in peace.

And sometimes, between a brother and a sister, that's the best you can hope for.

LOOK FOR BOOK 3 IN THE
MONSTERTOWN MYSTERY SERIES:

INVASION OF THE
SCORP-LIONS!

A Monstertown Mystery

THE ONLY THING more dangerous than a dare is a double-dog dare. Most kids I know are powerless to resist one, and Benny Brackman and I were no exceptions. That's why nighttime found us creeping around the school's mechanical room searching for a ghost—despite common sense, good judgment, and the risk of missing my favorite TV show.

"Darn Tyler Spork," said Benny. He shone his blacklight flashlight into a shadowy corner behind one of the massive boilers.

"We didn't *have* to take his dare," I said.

Benny gave me The Look. It could mean different

things at different times, but just then it meant *Stop being a total doofus, Carlos.*

"No, really," I said, playing my own flashlight beam over cobwebs big enough to snare a Buick. "What kind of fool deliberately risks supernatural danger, just on a dare?"

Benny smirked. "Have you looked in the mirror lately?"

He was right, so I ignored him.

I turned slowly, taking in the room. It was chilly and grim, smelling of dust, oil, and that funky wet-cat-with-gas odor we'd come to associate with whatever was haunting our school. The room was packed with pipes and ducts and mysterious machines. Darkness enfolded it, except for our lights and a faint red glow from the control boards.

The perfect place for a paranormal ambush.

The tiny hairs on my neck raised as my imagination kicked into gear. I pictured headless skeletons, leering monsters, creatures made of ectoplasm and raw, bloody flesh. (Yes, I watch too many movies.)

Something skittered behind a boiler.

"What was that?" I whipped around, aiming my flashlight toward the noise.

In the purplish-black light, Benny's eyes glowed as huge and white as brand-new volleyballs. "I d-dunno," he whispered. "Do ghosts make that kind of noise?"

"You've known me since kindergarten. Have I ever mentioned meeting a ghost?"

Slowly, ever so carefully, we crept past thick conduit

pipes that would've looked right at home in Dr. Frankenstein's laboratory. At the far edge of the boiler, Benny and I paused, gathering our courage.

He nodded, and together we peeked around the corner.

I gasped.

"Whoa!" cried Benny.

The creature captured in our flashlight beams was no ghost. No animated skeleton. In fact, it was so strange I couldn't wrap my mind around it.

The thing looked . . . wrong, somehow.

Roughly the size of a pit bull, it glowered up at us with the hungry amber stare of a big cat. Its head and muscular body resembled a lion, but two thick pincers, like those of a crab, curved forward from its chest, clicking and snapping. Segmented armor plates along the spine led to a thick scorpion tail, which arched forward, dripping poison.

Not exactly the kind of thing you want to meet in a dark room. Or even a well-lit one. My heart thudded so irregularly, it felt like it was beat-boxing.

The creature hissed, tail twitching.

Benny and I stumbled back.

"What the heck?" he rasped.

I backed into a pipe with a *thunk*. Behind us, another hiss.

"I'm not sure," I said, shining my light toward the sound, "but I think it's got a friend."

My beam found a second monster, right behind me.

It snarled, bared some serious fangs, and bowed its chest to the ground like a playful puppy. But this thing was no puppy.

"*¡Hijole!*" I swayed, off balance.

"Look out, Carlos!" cried Benny.

The creature's tail lashed forward at me. My feet seemed frozen in place, as its knife-sharp stinger plunged down, down . . .

Ugh, I've done it again. I started my story at an exciting spot, like our teacher always says to, but I forgot to mention a few important things. Like who Benny and I are. Like what's going on. And like how we ended up in a room full of monsters in the first place.

I don't know how authors do it; this writing stuff is *hard*.

Maybe I should take you back to the beginning. No, not to the day I was born. The day we realized that someone, or some*thing*, was terrorizing Monterrosa Elementary, and that someone (namely Benny and I) had to do something about it.

About the Author

Raised by wolves just outside Los Angeles, **BRUCE HALE** began his career as a writer while living in Tokyo, and continued it when he moved to Hawaii. Before entering the world of children's books, he worked as a magazine editor, toymaker, surveyor, corporate lackey, gardener, actor, and DJ.

From picture books to novels and graphic novels, Bruce has written and illustrated more than thirty-five books for kids, including his Chet Gecko Mysteries series and his School for S.P.I.E.S. trilogy: *Playing with Fire*, *Thicker Than Water*, and *Ends of the Earth*.

When not writing and illustrating, Bruce loves to perform. He has appeared onstage, on television, and in an independent movie called *The Ride*. Bruce is a popular speaker and storyteller for audiences of all ages. He has taught writing workshops at colleges and universities, and spoken at national conferences of writing, publishing, and literacy organizations. On top of that, Bruce has visited elementary schools across the country and internationally. (You'd never guess he loves to travel.)

These days, Bruce lives in Santa Barbara, California, with his wife, Janette, and his sweet mutt, Riley. When he's not at the computer or drawing board, you'll find him hiking the hills, bicycling, or riding the waves (when it's warm enough, that is). He also likes going to movies and performing jazz music.